A Dash of Crazy

B R Nash

Whiteley Publishing

© B R Nash 2013

Published by Whiteley Publishing Ltd
First paperback edition 2013

ISBN 978-1-908586-61-2

In The Beginning

I couldn't wait for my friends to turn up. There were four of us, we were never separated and did most things together. Today was a day for the woods at the back of my parents' house.

Jo-Jo turned up first and Mazy and Debs were only a few seconds behind.

"I'm off out, Mum!" I shouted as we all rushed for the front door to get out.

"I want you back at six for your tea… no later!" Mum shouted back trying to catch me before I left.

"OK!" We were gone; I had no intentions of being in for six.

As it was a Friday and a lovely sunny day we all decided to have a little private party in the woods. Debs had persuaded her brother to go to the local corner shop for a small selection of alcohol.

He brought us white lightening cider and this strange orange drink called 20/20. Jo-Jo had pinched four fags off her mum and I brought the music, a device that played tapes, called a ghetto blaster.

We walked the back way to the woods, avoiding going down my garden path. The last thing I wanted was Mum marching up to the woods to find me when she realised I was late for tea.

"WHERE IS SHE?" Dad was angry, we could hear him from our hide away shouting at mum.

OK, so I was late, it was half 6, we were all pissed as farts and hanging upside down in the trees, listening to hip hop.

From where I was hanging I could see my garden and I could see Mum stood, staring out of the kitchen window straight at us, whilst Dad stomped about from one room to the other. I knew she knew where I was, but I didn't care. My friends were more important to me than my obnoxious family. My mates were always there to listen and helped me wipe away my tears; all my parents did was create those tears.

Dad wasn't so perfect; he was having an affair with his secretary. I caught them shagging on his desk one day when I popped in to his office. It was his fault; he didn't lock the door but it was my fault I caught him. I was scolded, Dad made a bullshit story up to Mum and yet again, she believed him.

I knew it was wrong but I was too scared to break Mum's heart so I've carried this secret with me for years, but the only problem was me and my Dad never got on after that. My sister was his pride and joy, all I got was a nasty beating, each time he could find the slightest problem. So I rebelled, if he was going to treat me like shit to keep my mouth shut, then after a while I started behaving like it because nothing I did after that moment was ever right. I just gave up.

It was the love from Andy which saved me from destroying myself. We met in school as friends, but soon became an item just before we all left education and went our separate ways. I hoped that I would keep in touch with my best buddies, but they all had plans of their own and soon we saw less and less of each other, and I saw more of Andy.

My life felt complete with Andy. He made me feel special and loved me for who I was and not once did he try to change me. My Mum and Dad, however, were hugely disappointed in me. They always wanted more from me, I was never good enough and my perfect sister always had the praise. This is probably why, as siblings, I resented her. She had carved a fantastic future for herself and landed herself a rich doctor for a husband. With my sister a solicitor and Dad being a retired solicitor, how on earth could I compete? Only my Andy willingly gave me the love and respect I desperately craved.

"Why don't you go to college and make something of your life?" This was always Dad's question.

"You won't get anywhere with Andy, go and find yourself a decent boyfriend!" That was always from Mum.

Andy tried his hardest to fit in with my judgemental family. He was always aspiring to find the next big thing which would set us up for life. My parents doubted his ability though, maybe down to the fact that a couple of times we had to borrow money from them to cover Andy's new business ventures. Unfortunately they both failed, but I knew deep down he would have his day. What I didn't realise was that one day I would have mine.

1

I sat down to my bamboo table and chairs, basking in the summer sun; tea in one hand, book in the other. The garden looks perfect with pink roses lining the lawn, the herb gardens growing superbly next to my ornate water feature. Plump apples on the trees are ripening nicely and there's always plenty of fragrant lavender to pick for my window sills.

The gardens have matured with me; we've lived here nearly twenty years now. We had to start the garden from scratch, as it had overgrown with bramble and weeds. We needed somewhere for the children to play safely, without being torn apart by thorns. So renovations began with the garden and the cottage came second.

As I soak up the tranquillity of the flourishing garden, fond memories of me and Andy flooded into my mind. We'd had some laughs, pulling weeds and losing our balance. The garden was full of worthless treasures; we found crumpled bicycle wheels, tin cans, silver spoons and even an old boot along the way. The best bit was relieving our bruised bums with those hot soothing bubble baths.

It was only when we had gone part way through the digging that I came across a very unique brooch. I washed it in warm soapy water and after the mud had dissolved it came up brilliantly shiny. I liked it so much I kept it, a perfect reminder of the hard work and fun we had that summer. Where did it all go wrong? Maybe I will never know. The garden somehow doesn't seem so vibrant and enchanting anymore, the book becomes meaningless words across the page. Only the hot English tea remains unscathed. Empty, nothing but disappointment surrounding me.

"Hi, Mum." She made me jump.

I'm so caught up in my world of misdemeanours; she pounced on me unnoticed.

"Jesus, Chloe you scared me!"(But you also snapped me out of my mood.)

"Sorry, Mum." She giggles, dumping her bag on the floor and she slumps down in the chair next to me.

Chloe glares at me, almost trying to read my overactive mind. She instantly senses overwhelming sadness. She knows I've been trying my best since her dad left.

I had met Andy quite early in my life; at only eighteen I had fallen in love with a man five years my senior. Andy met all my requirements in a suitor; he was good looking, kind, romantic and a really good business man. We had scrimped and saved to buy our first house. I wanted a cottage in the village, so that's what we bought and we still own today. Andy's Internet business took off really well; there were a few problems with cash, bad business deals and lots of wasted time until eventually Andy hit the jack pot. He was a self made millionaire by the time he hit his 40th year. I refused to move from 'Holly Bush Cottage'. There was enough space; it was finely decorated, picturesque and comfortable, plus it was within walking distance to the children's school and my fond memories securely held me captive in this tireless village up until this day.

The money, however, changed Andy. He didn't want to live in this small village anymore. He craved more and it soon became evident that we both wanted different things from life. That's when the cracks began to show and this made me anxious when Andy was on his business trips. I started to notice subtle changes in his behaviour, such as a change of aftershave, new designer underwear and unexplained transactions on bank statements.

At first I put it down to his midlife crisis, or the need to retain his youth. Journeys to the dry cleaners got more frequent; especially after his trips and I was no longer required to do his laundry. His shirts were immaculate, his tailored suit collection grew and his favourite designer 'Armani' was on speed dial.

All this was too much for me, including the unexpected trip to America which was ONLY supposed to be for a week, which ended up being for a month. His phone calls and emails became less and less freqent, the details of his meetings and deals created were skipped over and he never admitted to anything. I did know there was something wrong, the only thing left was to ask him outright.

"Please tell me, Andy." Desperately, I pleaded with my new designer bloke.

"There's nothing to tell, Pol, I shouldn't be too much longer. Why you don't invite your best mate round for a few days, just until I manage to get home." His voice was flat and I knew there was something on his mind.

"Just how long, Andrew?" Silence.

"Andrew!" Desperate for an answer, my anger heightened.

"FOR GODS SAKE... ANDREW, ANSWER ME!" The lid came off my anger. Shaking, I knew he would either put the phone down, or twist the story and leave me feeling bad for getting angry in the first place. To my surprise it was neither.

"I will book my flight back tomorrow... we need to chat, can you get your mum to take the kids on Saturday? That's three days from now." Andrew was very businesslike and matter of fact.

11

"Andy… what's wrong, what do we need to chat about?" This was serious. I knew it was going to be about our relationship. We were not married, as he would never commit to me. This pained me as I never felt good enough for him even though he always said I was his everything, but it had always felt like there was something missing.

"Nothing, Polly, we will discuss it when I'm back… OK!"

"OK… bye then, love ya." There was no reply, just the click of the phone line. I stood in the kitchen staring at the phone, utterly shocked. He never replied! Dumbfounded, I replaced the receiver. It was time for a cuppa. Tea was my answer for everything.

I watched as Andy, now known as HIM, packing his belongings. His designer suits were neatly placed into suit bags, his Italian leather shoes put into crocodile skin boxes. Everything was so meticulous and in order. It was not the Andy I knew, hence the name HIM. Boy, had he changed!

Yes, the advantage of not having to worry about money is nice, but it does have its draw backs. This is one of them. He met another woman in America. It wasn't on his last trip, he had been a few times before, but only stayed for week intervals and the wench (his new lover) worked for another company that he was doing business with.

"Do you want a cup of tea?"

I asked, trying to delay HIM from leaving too quickly. I so needed answers, knowing that if he went now I would be struggling to gain any info at all.

"Erm… yeah OK, but I haven't got long."

A business associate was due to fetch HIM in an hour, apparently he was staying at his place until things were sorted. I entered the bedroom with two cups of tea and a small plate of chocolate digestives, I knew this was a firm favourite of his.

"Thanks." His tone was dull.

I seized the moment, knowing my time was limited.

"Why?" My voice begged, caressing my favourite mug, as a tear rolled down my face.

Andy sighed, "You really want to know?" He raised his eyebrows in disbelief, slightly belittling my question.

Unable to find words, I just nodded. Andy looked at me and pity crossed his face. I'd been his partner and raised his children. That's all I was to him, a partner just like a work colleague. He said jump and I said how high, but that's how he liked it… control, his needs always came first, his excuse was "It's for the family… for all of us."

"Pol… I don't love you anymore, I'm grateful for your help and support over the last twenty years and they have been hard ones. I need change now and the fact is I've got money that allows me to do that. I've taken the chance to lead the life I've always dreamed of. I know you don't want the same life as I do."

I broke down, he had actually confirmed to me that my suspicions where right, I never was really good enough for him. This explains why we never had that beautiful wedding I always dreamed of. If it had ever been all worked out, every finest detail had been secretly written down in my diary. I knew the dress and style, bridesmaids, cake, the reception and a selection of guests to invite. My hidden dream was shattered; our life had been a fake. And for what? So he could make his millions… and use me along the way? So he could keep his lovely family life if it all went wrong? But it hasn't gone wrong. Well, not for HIM anyway.

"Mum, everything will be OK." Chloe reaches out and holds my hand.

I turn to Chloe, "You're right, come on let's grab a cup of tea."

Chloe smiles to herself.

I always calm down with a brew. She follows me into the kitchen. Hanging up her bag, she sits at the oak table, twisting her fingers underneath to hide her nervousness (Only a few more minutes until her dad rings). Eager and patient she waits for me to relax a little.

Her dad has asked her to accompany him to London for five days, for some catch up time. She knows it will upset me, but she has to tell me. The planned trip is a week from Friday; it's also the same weekend her dad left, so it will have repercussions. Yes, I will be miserable, and left on my own. Josh will be off on a camping trip with his school, so it will be just me, myself and I. Choosing her moment wisely with ten minutes to spare, Chloe just blurts it out.

"Oh right... OK." My mood deflates again. "He is your dad, so you will have fun. Don't worry about me. I will be fine."

Chloe glares at me in disbelief. A moment ago she was sad and now she doesn't seem to care. Reading my daughters reaction, I sip my tea and proceed, "Just because me and your dad have split, it doesn't mean he's split from you. It sounds fun. Will you ring me when you arrive there? I want to know you're safe?"

"Yeah, course I will, I promise." Checking out the time, Chloe pushes on, "Dad's going to call me in two minutes, to check if it's OK with you." She mumbles whilst sipping her tea, trying to be blasé.

"Chloe, its fine... just call me, OK?" I said making my excuses as I left the kitchen.

As I sat in my bedroom, memories of Andy's leaving day flood back. Avoiding the big man's phone call, I scan the room. Realisation hit me, I've not even changed anything. The room is exactly as it was that day nearly one year ago. Holy cow! It will be one year next weekend and I will have to see him! Sitting at the dressing table I stared at my weathered reflection. Rummaging around in the dresser drawer I find a pink headband. Scraping my hair off my face, I start pulling at my skin, trying to smooth out the lines around my eyes, running my fingers over my brows.

"I need to do something about this; I haven't changed a thing, the room or myself. It is time for a change."

My reflection just looks at me with a grin on her face. She's been waiting for these words and she knows Polly means business. "Hurray

Hurray!" She gives herself a pat on the back for helping me to notice my own reality.

OK, so what now? So I'm not good enough... well, maybe, I've gained a few pounds over the last 10 years, but I did mother your children and OK, so I've a got a couple of grey hairs and a small map of England growing on my forehead, but that doesn't mean there's anything wrong with me... or does it? I suppose my bobbed hair doesn't work for me either and so what if I like to wear the colour brown, what's wrong with that? Hmm, I need to make a list, not just any list, but one about me, the way I look, my future and how I'm going to get my own life back. Revenge... yes that's the answer, sweet revenge. I will change, you will see... but when I have, it will be too late. I will make the rules and this time you can obey them, you think you've won... but you lost by leaving me... men, do they actually know anything? You think you know better than a woman, REALLY, I mean, do you really understand how powerful women are? It's not all about money, you know... just wait and see.

Overhearing Chloe saying her byes to HIM on the phone, I reached for my bedside drawer, locating a pen and a note book. Sitting on my patchwork quilt, I wasted no time on the beginnings of list number one.

2

"Glad that's over." I said out loud.

Chloe had just left for London with her dad. He was his usual neatly pressed, highly scented self. Me... well, I wore brown, just to annoy him. Glancing at my dressing table mirror, I caught a smile staring back at me. As I was finishing off packing my overnight bag, I found my iPod, relieved I had found it and so I threw it in for some entertainment.

The weather outside was partially sunny, my over worrying side tells me that my brown ankle length dress could get chilly so I locate a nice long brown cardigan from Chloe's wardrobe. I took a moment to admire some of Chloe's clothes. Beautiful summer dresses line the built in wardrobe, cute little cardigans, brightly coloured sandals with toe posts, they've always amused me.

Yes, they look nice. But surely they can't be comfortable? Taking one dress I liked, I wandered over to her full length mirror. Putting the hanger over my head gently pulling the garment around my figure, I notice the warm oranges seem to light up my face, that familiar woman in the reflection seems to agree, as she's smiling at me.

As I lock the back door, I gaze at my beautiful garden. It all seems so real now. This is it; my new life begins starting today. Carefully, I ushered all the wooden chairs to their correct position. Glancing at the clock I calculated that Chloe should be in London by now. It's been four hours since she left with her dad. Grabbing my mobile, I begin to text her. Stopping midway, I delete the text hoping that she will contact me like she promised. Searching through my phone I start to re-read the texts I had from Andy, most are matter of fact,

'Will be with you in ten mins, make sure Josh is ready.'

'Cheque is in the post.' (That's maintenance then)

'Pick your papers up tomoz from solicitors.' Hmmm the cottage.

Andy, out of guilt, gave me the cottage, along with all the furniture and my fiesta. He put all of it in my name, as we were not married, so I didn't stand a chance on much, but his words, 'it's for the kids', were his justification to the mess he left me in. Lucky for me all of it was paid off early.

"Hi, Mum." Chloe called, as I was deciding whether to delete his crappy messages.

"Hi sweetie, did you get there safely?" Pleased that she interrupted me.

"Yeah, Mum. We got here over an hour ago. Dad took me for a latte, because he said he wanted to tell me something… and now he wants me to tell you..." Her voice trailed off, "what he's just told me."

Chloe paused.

"What is it Chloe… you sound puzzled, is everything OK?"

In proper Chloe style she just came out with it, "Mum… Dad's getting married, he's marrying the wench!" She sounded shocked.

"Mum?"

"I heard you, darling." (I don't know what to say… he's marrying that wench!). Forcing back the tears, my voice becomes choked.

"Dad wants me to meet her in an hour. She wants me to be a bridesmaid and Josh a page boy."

After the conversation ends, anger compels me. I turn off my mobile and by impulse I throw it against the kitchen wall. It breaks into several pieces. My body crumples on the brown leather sofa, unable to move. The bastard, the dirty rotten bastard. So much for Mr-I-don't-do-marriage-or-commitment. I uncontrollably sob, crying out years of pain and regret into my hands. My heart is shattered; making me curl up into a ball as I hug myself tight for the next hour hoping it will help ease the lost feeling. With my little trip this afternoon I need to stay focused. No bailing out now, it's too late. With a drained bank account and a must for change, I'm aware of what I have to do, it has to be done and even more so for my determination to prove HIM wrong.

Feeling completely wasted and empty, I check in at a guest house in Manchester City. The room is comfortable with frilly bedspreads and lamp shades, shades of pink and green cover the walls and behind the door is a gilt full length mirror. Dumping my luggage on the floor I head for the quaint shower.

The water is hot and very refreshing after my train journey. I wrap my freshly washed hair in a pink fluffy towel and wrap myself in my dressing gown. Walking into the bedroom, I attempt to figure out all these different emotions of the past six hours and turn to the mirror. Emotionless, I unravel out of my gown; standing naked, I gaze at my forty year old body.

I caress my soft stomach, as fond memories of giving birth wash over me. I smile as I slide my hand towards my full breasts. A slight stroke instantly makes my nipples erect and a moan escapes my lips.

It's been a long time since I've been touched. Allowing my hand to wander further I gently ease fingers through pubic hair, sensing the springy sensations tingling the secret weapon, as desires overcome me and I tease open my vagina, lightly touching my silky smooth lips. With one hand on my breast, I flick a nipple, oozing moisture from need, I insert a finger inside. Closing my eyes, I envision a good looking young man slowly seducing me, making me heighten with lust. I slowly move my hand from the erect nipple leading down to my throbbing need, as I gently touched and circle my button, electricity overcomes me and the vibrations of orgasm control me. I drops to the floor, glancing at the woman in the mirror. The reflection looks pleased and purrs with contentment.

A while later, I knock at the door and I wait patiently, slightly apprehensive and feeling fresh from my new found delights.

"Hello, do come in." A nice friendly woman beckons me towards the clinic waiting room.

"Hi and thanks." I give her my name and she ticks me off her clip board.

"Would you like coffee or tea?"

"Tea please, no sugar. Thank you." At last a cup of tea, at least that will keep me calm. Sipping my tea I forage through the pile of unwanted lifestyle magazines, something caught my eye. "Hmmm, I've got one of those." I quickly turn my head to see if anyone noticed my outburst, phew! I was safe. A big advert was shouting at me in big red letters,

'Antiques Wanted For Auction.' That's when I first saw my brooch, the one I found in my garden. Wow, I wonder… is it an antique? It could be worth something. A new car springs to mind and then a holiday. I must find out how to go about this. I carefully and quietly tear the page out, checking no one's looking and place it securely into my bag.

"Polly Perkins?" Oh no! I think the receptionist caught me.

"Polly Perkins?" She asked again, "Your appointment with Dr Hash?"

"Yes, that's me." I tried hard not to giggle, I'm a daft sod and realise she is calling me for my appointment, not the stealing of a magazine page.

I followed the receptionist into Dr Hash's room. My fear completely disappeared as my thoughts returned to the brooch and the excitement of its possible worth. Even though I didn't know its origin I had a feeling, a gut instinct it was going to be good.

"All done, Mrs Perkins." I was that sucked into my own thoughts that I'd not realised my treatment had finished.

"Thank you." I replied and smiling, I collected my belongings and left the room.

I must have worried for nothing, that didn't hurt at all. Feeling inspired, I wandered around Manchester looking for a reputable hairdressers and that was just the beginning. Clothes shopping, shoe shopping, the possibilities are endless, but first my hair then my nails. I sense my inner being smiling, this is going to be a good couple of days and a new me to go with it.

After my big day of change, I decided to grab a take away and head for the guest house. I snuck my food upstairs and flopped on the bed totally exhausted but extremely happy. Carefully I opened my Chinese take away, whilst taking massive mouthfuls and eating too quickly, I accidently dropped Chow Mein down my chin. I grabbed a tissue and stood in front of the gilt mirror, horror washed over me "God, that looks awful!" I was covered. Well, I did like my food, maybe a little too much. What a state I was in, I vowed to my reflection that I would eat healthy and more regular from now on. I knew I needed to lose a few pounds, so I decided that this take away meal would be my last for the next couple of months. 'I will be slimmer', I told myself, glad that no one could see the slobbering mess I was in. Quickly, I grabbed my mobile and took a picture of my reflection before I wiped my mouth and chin clean, a good reminder of my last junk meal to help my slimming process, I decided to get it developed and place the evidence on my fridge at home.

Back home I retrieved my list of change, whilst ticking off the boxes I assessed my achievements.

No.1 Get my hair done, style and colour.

No.2 Buy some vibrant clothes in up to date styles.

No.3 Get my nails done.

No.4 Sort out a facial and eyebrows.

No.5 Book an appointment with the clinic.

No.6 LOSE weight must get into a size 10 in the next 2 months. (Join a gym?)

No.7 Clear out my wardrobe, take the brown items to the charity shop.

No.8 Redecorate my bedroom.

No.9 Buy a new bed.

No.10 Find a sexy new man, preferably younger than me and full of experience.

Well, I managed to tick five of the 10, so I picked up the laptop hoping to find inspiration for 8 and 9. I felt inspired to change the colour of my room, none of it really matched. I also located a local decorator to piece all my ideas together and booked him in as soon as possible, so that made two more boxes ticked off!

Making a cup of tea, I realised I'd forgotten my flooring, so scanning the internet again I came across some fabulous offers on wooden flooring. That's what I needed; only a touch of brown, it is a hard colour for me to give up and it will go nicely with the greens and creams. Still feeling creative, I ordered some green and pink bedding with matching curtains and a couple of scatter cushions. All my furniture was white so it should all match really well.

Happy with my purchases, I closed the laptop down, taking my tea upstairs with me I went loaded with bin liners to empty my wardrobe and drawers. This was an impossible task, as my keep pile was bigger than my chuck pile. I do like to save things for a rainy day, so I decided to put my keep pile in the loft (just in case I 'needed' them).

I laid all my nice new clothes on my bed, lined the collection of shoes and sandals I had bought on the floor and placing my hands on my hips I glanced at the mirror. I glanced again and again, is that really me? Wow, even I was pleased. Not just the purring pussy cat of a woman looking back at me, now I was getting excited at the return of Chloe and Josh, as their reaction would be fun. I just hoped they approved of the new sophisticated me.

Closing the bedroom door behind me, I stopped dead. Oh God, I nearly forgot the advert I had torn out of the magazine! I ran down the stairs, frantically emptying the contents of my bag onto the kitchen table. "Got it!" Jumping with excitement I leaped upstairs to check the brooch and the photo likeness. "Yes! Yes! Yes!" Skipping around my bedroom in full excitement. "Laptop!" I ran back down stairs, impatiently waiting for the damn thing to load; now it's time for a valuation. I wonder what it's worth?

3

"Wow, Mum!" Chloe and Josh both stood amazed.

"You approve then?" I said, hoping that was the right choice of words.

"Mum, you look really... young and sexy." Josh smiled at me, unsure if his words would be justified.

"Thank you, sweetheart." I instantly gave my beautiful children a massive hug.

After dinner, Chloe and Josh went through the activities they did with their father; Josh had already been informed of his dad's forthcoming wedding. They both seemed really pleased, which helped me to accept the 'Wench and HIM' a tiny bit more. Even though I've cut my feelings of love for HIM, it still hurts how he just had no respect for me and jumped into bed with the first available 'bit of stuff' that came along. Well, that's what I presume, if I think too much about it I could master a thousand different times I've had 'that feeling' knowing something was wrong.

"Kids, I've got another surprise for you!" Grinning I sat In front of the fire, whilst they both sat on the sofa waiting for me to begin.

"I've been on a little trip. I went to Manchester for a massive makeover when you were away. So as you have noticed, I've gone blonde and had some hair extensions, had my eyebrows done and a full set of French nails. I've cleared my wardrobe out and purchased lots of new clothes and accessories to match, I did have help from the sales assistant." Laughing, I proceeded.

"But there's one thing that has had a massive effect on our lives or it will do soon." Chloe and Josh sit patiently, waiting for my announcement.

"I went to have a chemical peel and some Botox to freshen my face and whilst in the clinic, I found this." I held out the advert about the Auction House.

"What does it mean, Mum?" Josh asked, looking puzzled.

"Well," I hand out the brooch and watched their puzzled faces turn into greatly surprised ones.

"Does this mean its valuable then?" Chloe comes straight to the point.

"Yes… it is, in fact I've already put it in the auction." I was waiting for it.

"HOW MUCH?" They both shouted in excitement.

Giggling at my two precious children, I couldn't speak. Chloe and Josh sat on the floor next to me eagerly waiting for me to respond.

"This brooch is worth… two million English pounds." Christ, saying it out loud sounds so amazing.

"TWO MILLION?" They both screamed down my ear.

"We're richer than Dad now!" Chloe exclaims, and I sat there open mouthed, I had never thought about that. Oh, what a turnaround! Maybe it's time to make another list.

Looking at my last list I realised I'd forgotten about number 10… a new fella. 'But how am I going to do that?' I ask myself. I never met anyone new; my life consisted of kids, work, pottery classes and weekly meet ups with my friends for a local pub lunch. Hmmm. "Maybe I need a new hobby? Or I could join a gym?"

Flashes Of intimidating meatheads pumping iron and dainty fitness girls plastered in makeup, wiggling their tight asses on the cardio machines cross my mind. Deciding against that, I boot up the laptop for some much needed inspiration. Typing in the search engine 'ways to attract a young man' was how I started. OK, so I was feeling brave. Rows and rows of dating sites came up.

Looking at the first on the list, it looked familiar. Then it hit me. I remembered catching HIM on this site, but of course he had denied it, but I suspect every man would. Being naive, I believed his 'spam mail' plea. What a fool, Polly! I told myself, shaking my head. Feeling a challenge, I logged onto the site. If I joined I bet I could find HIM. Grabbing a piece of paper and a pen, I started working on my profile, as it had to be perfect.

"Lady in her 40th year looking for a respectable younger man for fun times and friendship." Not convinced on that one I tried again.

"Sexy Mature Lady seeks younger Play Mate." Nope, that makes me sound over 60 and cheap.

"Fun Loving, Sensual Feline WLTM Younger Intelligent Male for Times to Remember." Liking that one, I made it my catch line and then carried on filling out all the boring details about my life. I decided to lie about my work status, as the term 'Shelf Stacker at Graham's Grocers' didn't quite fit, so I entered entrepreneur, knowing that I would be doing some type of business with my new found wealth.

Happy with my answers, I had to upload a picture. Scrolling through my picture album; they all were very 'brown'. I needed a fresh one of my new look. I decided to use the web cam, but my face came out distorted and then I became cyclops, my head shrunk at the top and went fat at the bottom… damn kids! They've been playing with the settings for distorted images. The mobile it is then.

Remembering when I watched Chloe pose in front of her mirror, with side poses and pouts, I began to give it a go. Chloe always told me you have to find your best side… well, it took me an hour to figure it out and over a hundred deleted photos, until I finally got my shot. I was impressed; I wore bright colours and enough make up without over doing it, as I needed to be natural.

Uploading the photo, I began to tap my nails on the table, the wait was tormenting me. A few seconds later, my perfect new image appeared on the screen. Oh God, I ran my finger over the enter button. Hesitating, I closed my eyes and pressed send. 'Your profile is completed' popped up across the screen. I logged onto my own profile, checking my handy work. All of it read really well and I was amused at my little catch line on my 'looking for' page.

"Dark handsome younger man wanted, must be a business person, able to make me laugh and possess the ability to SURPRISE me." Slightly nervous on the thoughts of my fantasy, I hastily reached for the kettle… time for a cup of tea.

I had barely put the milk in my tea when the phone rang.

"Hello, I would like to speak with Mrs Polly Perkins, please." The posh voice spoke with authority.

"That's me, who's speaking please?"

"Good Afternoon Mrs Perkins, this is Mr Summers from the auction house Hale and Hale. I'm pleased to inform you that your brooch sold this morning. If you would like to pop down to see us, we need to complete the necessary paper work, with two forms of ID such as a passport or driving license and an up to date utility bill plus your bank details and then we can transfer the money to your chosen account immediately."

Gosh, where has my head been for the last couple of hours? I had forgotten about the brooch! "OK, yes, that would be great. What time's best for you?" The information was starting to register.

"And how much did the brooch sell for?" Excited, I located a pen, waiting for details.

"We're open until 5pm today, so anytime until then will be fine." Mr Summer's deep throaty voice was hurried.

"OK, thank you, I will be round today then." Damn! I never got a

26

price, oh well I'm sure it will be a nice surprise and I do like surprises.

As the kids were off school for the holidays I decided to make it a family trip, so on my way I fetched Josh from his swimming lesson and Chloe from her friend's house. Excited, they both raced into the car.

"How much, Mum?" Chloe was so impatient.

"Don't know, sweetie, Mr Summers didn't say." I glanced at Josh.

"You OK, Josh?" His face was ashen.

"Yep, Dad rang me." He fidgeted on the back seat.

"OK... what's wrong?" I tried to sound calm.

"Dad wants me to stay with him until the wedding's over." Josh mumbled, scared of my response.

"WHAT!" Chloe butted in again. "He's not asked me!" She scowled.

"What did you tell him, Josh?" I said amazed and Josh noticed my eyes widen.

"That I would talk to you first." Pleased with himself, he slumped on the seat.

"Shall we discuss this later over dinner?"

"Yeah, OK Mum." Josh was no longer ghostly.

Josh was fifteen and due to go into his last year of senior school and was on his summer break. He was quite immature for his age and he got bullied a lot at school, so maybe this might do him some good. His sister towered over his small plump frame, as she was more like her dad, with long black hair and very statuesque. At seventeen she was due to start art college and maybe that's why 'Him' didn't ask her. I figured that Josh's dad could help out a little. Josh was always moaning about his ginger hair, I thought it was beautiful, but maybe I should let him grow up a bit and take him to the hairdressers for a treat. Chloe always managed to squeeze something out of me, but Josh never really asked for much.

"Do you want to get your hair dyed, Josh?"

"REALLY?" He screamed "You would let me?" Astounded Josh bolted up right in the car.

"Why not, if it makes you happy... but as long as you promise me, you won't tell your Dad about the 'money'... OK?"

"Yeah, that's cool, Mum... thanks." Josh relaxed, happy at his new revelation.

Chloe glared at me out of the corner of her eyes. I winked at her, I had something up my sleeve for her as well and she got the message and returned to singing along to the tunes on the radio.

"In the next 100 metres take the 3rd exit."

"Approaching the roundabout take the 3rd exit."

"Take the exit."

"MUM!" The kids both shouted. The voice from the sat nav fell on deaf ears and the kids woke me up.

I swerved on to the slip road just in time; I really do have to stop thinking about my advert on the dating site, if only I could put my brain in the freezer to stop my thoughts for one day. I stopped the car outside Hale and Hale, located the car park at the rear of the building and pulled in to a nice wide space next to a top of the range Aston Martin. Josh had to check out the car, looking through all the windows, standing a distance behind it, walking to the front of it, to me he was being nosey, to him it was his dream car and it had to be admired. We sat and waited in the reception area and then Mr Summers greeted us.

"Welcome, Mrs Perkins, I'm Mr Summers." He shook my hand, greeted the children and escorted us to the office at the back.

The office was huge; the walls were lined with wooden panels, tall yucca plants stood in the bay windows. Heavy wine coloured velvet curtains lined the windows along with pictures of the company's success stories spaced evenly on the walls. The children were invited to sit on the red Chesterfield couch. I was shown to the chair next to the desk.

Papers were stacked in an orderly fashion; he had a picture of his family at the side of his Apple Mac computer and a picture of the Aston Martin on the wall behind his boardroom chair. The same car that I had just parked next to. Whilst we were waiting for Mr Summers to collect all the paper work, I accepted the kind offer of a hot drink; the kids had hot chocolate and a chocolate digestive.

I couldn't help noticing how beautiful Mr Summers looked. He sounded much older on the phone, but voices are very deceptive. I took a peek at his family photo, his wife looked really young and he had two small boys. He can't be that old? Assessing the evidence I would guess he was around 30 at the most.

"Welcome to Hale and Hale. Mr Hale himself wanted to be here, but his wife is ill in hospital so he couldn't make it, so he left the exchange with me... please, do call me Gabriel, Mrs Perkins." He held out his hand again before lowering that pert backside on to his chair.

"Gabriel, very nice to meet you, please call me Polly." I blushed, head in the clouds as usual.

The kids giggled. I threw them a quick 'shut up stare' and they quit immediately. Softly spoken, Gabriel revealed how much we had made, Chloe and Josh were hard to contain and they were bouncing on the Chesterfield sofa. With my mind in a state of shock, I failed to restrain them. Oh well if they broke it, I could afford to replace it.

"Thank you very much." I smiled Cheshire cat style, shaking Gabriel's hand. He smiled back, his eyes soft and inviting. If he wasn't attached I would have planted a big kiss on his cheek, but instead he caught me off guard. He paused from shaking my hand and looked deeply into my eyes across the dark oak and leather desk and slowly raised my hand to his full soft lips.

He gently kissed my skin, sending shivers down my curves around my body, all the time not breaking our eye contact. Shocked, I spun my head round to see if the kids had noticed. They were still bouncing and screaming on the red leather sofa, completely unaware. Blushing from the neck up I retrieved my hand slowly, feeling where his kiss had brushed my skin. I took a deep breath and calmed the children down.

Wow! A lot has been achieved today and this man before me is placing the cherry on the top.

4

Josh checked out the Aston Martin once again when we were in the car park.

"Can we get one of those, please, Mum?" His pupils widened.

"Now, Josh, just because we have money to spend, doesn't mean I'm going to waste it."

Josh just looked at me, opened the car door and climbed into the back.

"Don't go getting greedy on me, Josh; we're still the same people."

He just sat looking out of the side window with his arms crossed. Chloe fastened her seat belt, I could tell she was quiet for a reason, I knew she was planning what to buy, even though it was my money, she always had plans for it.

We stopped off at this medieval type of pub, as the menu looked varied and reasonably priced. Inside the smell of steak filled the room and a friendly welcome made us stay, it was truly inviting and homely. Chloe ordered steak, Josh and I agreed it was a good choice and ordered the same.

After eating, I made my way to the ladies room to freshen up. I splashed water on my face and my make up slid down my cheeks making me look like a zombie. Taking my baby wipes out of my bag I looked again and my reflection caught my attention. I cocked my head to one side in disgust with my wrecked face paint and disapprovingly wagged a finger at my own reflection.

Oh dear, I'm slipping back to the brown me! I took a moment to gather myself, all this new found life was over whelming and Mr Summers, well... what on earth happened there? The reflection smiled at me, she approved of Mr Summers.

"Mum, are you ready?" Chloe poked her head round the bathroom door.

"Yes, I'm coming now." I handed her the car keys.

After I paid for the meal I took a business card, you never know when I might need to come here again and hopefully I will.

Back home Chloe yet again went round to her friends and Josh went playing in the woods, so I put my feet up to reflect on our trip. So much has happened in the last three weeks limiting my time; I bet my friends think I've deserted them, so I decided to arrange a lunch with Ellie my best friend. Tomorrow night was set, not lunch but a night out, so hopefully it won't be too busy as it was Friday and the town was always dead on Fridays.

Ellie stood at my front door, beautiful as ever. She wore a gold chiffon knee length dress with a small black belt and shiny black heels. Her hair was bright red and had been delicately curled making it look shiny and healthy. She looked a master piece.

"Come in, Ellie, no need to knock." She entered and gave me a super tight hug, and stood back looking amazed at the new me.

"Wow, Polly, you look fab!" Her mouth dropped.

"Do you like?" I asked teasingly doing a twirl.

My dress was an orange maxi dress with white lilies around the bottom. It had thin straps that helped lift my middle aged bust. I wore gold sandals and had curled the bottoms of my new blonde streaked hair,

I decided on the natural look with a touch of sexiness.

"Like! I love it, all of it, your hair, and your dress… your face looks… so pretty. Looks like I've got some hot competition tonight. When did you get so in with it, have you lost weight, too? You need to fill me in, the taxi is outside. Are you ready?" Typical Ellie, she always asks a thousand questions in one sentence.

"OK, I'm ready." I quickly glanced into the living room mirror, the tigress was giving me the seal of approval; happy with Ellie's reaction, I was ready for a night on the tiles.

Town was busier than normal and there were the young girls wearing killer heels and extremely short tight dresses, heavily plastered in make-up and walking with that sexy wiggle, always arm in arm. Young lads with gelled hair, that stank of aftershave, being oh so loud, whistling at the groups of young girls. People in fancy dress, one for a 30th birthday and a group of lads dressed as Smurfs. Then I remembered it was the summer holidays, no wonder it was so busy. This was my first night out since me and 'HIM' had split.

After I first split with Andy, Ellie decided I needed a pick me up tonic and took me out to get me sloshed. I just ended up in a mess, crying all night and vowed I wouldn't do that again until I was over him. It was a total waste of money and effort, so I had stayed in for the last year. Yet tonight I was ready to party, have fun and maybe by chance pull a nice young man.

We decided to go to the cocktail bar first, a firm favourite of Ellie's. At the back of the room was a man playing the piano, the walls were decorated in cream with brown swirls and dimly lit gold lanterns hung above the many window seats creating a relaxed ambiance.

Being a sophisticated bar it stopped the younger folk from coming in and it did have an over 21 policy. We ordered two margaritas with the young suited barman and he carefully turned the glasses over and dipped them in something like sugar, poured in the drink and added fresh fruit and a sparkly umbrella and they looked fab.

Ellie found a vacant window seat and elegantly sat down in the booth, I followed trying to copy her, but my skills of being lady like are still to be discovered. I had a feeling this was going to be a long night and there was so much I hadn't told her and she normally has a few tales to tell me, as Ellie was easily excitable. I thought tonight wouldn't be a good time to tell her about the money. Knowing Ellie's reaction, the whole pub would know, too.

We got the 'local gossip' talk out of the way and moaned about men. Even though Ellie was married, she never said a good word about her spouse. I told her about Andy's forthcoming wedding and the kids staying with him for a month, I explained about my trip of change and the fact I'd discovered myself again sexually. She was thrilled, Ellie was always very open about sex with me and she then proceeded to tell me how her other half only ever wanted anal sex with her. She was amazed that I got rid of the 'brown' clothes and that I'd changed my room and bed.

"You're all set to have another man in your life, Polly." She announced with a smile.

"Yes, I'm scared though."

I also told her about the dating site. She got her smart phone out and got me to log in; I had twenty four new messages. Ellie's inner child kicked in as she started clapping uncontrollably in excitement.

"Read them, quickly! I want to see!"

"OK, Jesus! I didn't think I would get that many." Nervously I opened the first one.

"Hi there, my name's Mike, I'm willing to please you whenever you want and I can surprise you when I take my trousers off."

"Ooh… that's gross!" I deleted him and looked at the next one.

"Hey sexy, would love to meet you, can't surprise you though, I'm skint." I hit the delete button.

Ellie thought this was highly amusing. I carried on.

"Hey, my name's Jason, I'm 19 and would love a chance for you to surprise me." Delete!

"Hi, my name's Mark. I'm a little older than you. Please check out my profile, I'm a business man only after a little fun. I don't want a relationship, but I am very eager to please and I'm full of surprises"... Save.

"Carry on." Ellie was highly amused at my expense.

Whilst we were in our own world, we failed to recognise how busy the bar had become. I made my excuses and went to the ladies room. The queue was horrendous; so unable to wait, I slipped into the men's room. I used to do this when I was eighteen and the men seemed to love it, but if the bouncers caught you, you were thrown out.

I quickly opened the door and shut it behind me putting my back to it. I quickly checked the urinals, good it was empty. I went in the cubicle and locked the door. The bathroom door went a couple of times and I could hear men unzipping their flies doing there business and leaving. Not one washed their hands! I was about to leave, thinking the coast was clear when I bumped into a good looking man on leaving the cubicle. I went bright red.

"Sorry." I said in a little girl voice.

"It's OK, Polly; I believe we have met before." I looked up.

"Shit!" I put my hand over my mouth at my inappropriate word. "Hello again, Mr Summers."

My heart started thumping in my throat; he smelt divine and looked so heavenly.

He laughed, "You look beautiful, Polly, it was very nice to see you again, even if it was in the men's room."

"I'm sorry; shall we make it the ladies next time?" Damn, that was sarcastic, but Gabriel laughed.

"Now that's a date I can't refuse."

I smiled and escaped the intoxicating smell of Mr Summers. Flustered,

I returned to my seat. Ellie had ordered us two more cocktails, these ones were blue.

"Sex on the beach." Ellie claimed, winking at me. Unsure of the secrecy, I gave her the 'what you up to look'. She handed me her phone. Damn, I didn't sign out and she'd been very busy surveying my messages, one in particular.

"Hello to you, I'm an Italian man of 29, I do aim to please my ladies. I'm a business man working in England for the next three months, so if you wish to go out for a lovely meal, please reply."

It was very vague; so I gathered that was down to his lack of English humour or lingo. Ellie had replied to him on my behalf.

"Thank you for your message, I would be delighted to escort you on an evening out. I'm in Lugo's cocktail bar at the moment, so if I don't reply straight away please forgive me. Look forward from hearing from you xx."

"For God's sake, Ellie!" I was slightly annoyed, but also slightly excited, I probably would have never replied to any of them.

"Chill out, woman, I knew you wouldn't reply so I took the liberty of doing it for you."

"True… but, can we talk about something else now?" I was wishing she would change the subject.

"Most definitely chick… that hunk over there keeps looking at me." Suddenly Ellie sat upright twiddling with her curls and cocking her head to one side. Someone had grabbed her attention. I looked up and there at the bar stood Gabriel, with a delicious looking friend. He noticed me looking and smiled with a sideways nod of 'hello'.

"Polly, did you see that... Polly, look he acknowledged me." Ellie spoke through gritted teeth.

Of course I didn't want to spoil her fun, so I kept quiet and allowed her to think Gabriel was putting his attention on her. The nice suited barman walked over to us carrying a tray with two slim champagne glasses. He stood in front of the table and placed the glasses down each one on to a coaster.

"What are these for?" Ellie quizzed him.

At that same moment Gabriel came over with an ice bucket and a well chilled bottle.

"Champagne!" Ellie's eyes lit up.

"Congratulations, Polly, this is to help you and your friend celebrate your good news."

"Oh… thank you, now I wasn't expecting that, thank you very much."

He returned back to his friend and his delicious smell lingered at our table.

Ellie's mouth dropped, "You know him? And what's he on about, what news? Polly… what haven't you told me?" She sounded stern.

I ignored her, poured us both a drink then raised my glass to my new friend. He raised his glass back and our gazes locked; I felt an enormous pull to the man I had only met a few days ago. I was unsure of why he would be around this area; it had taken me almost two hours to drive to meet him the other day. Maybe Ellie's theory is right, there's no such thing as coincidences, maybe he's meant to be in my life somewhere. Feeling confused and agitated by this wonderful man, I downed my drink and tried to think of a feasible lie for Ellie.

5

My story worked, she bought it but continued to ask me question after question. I made out that Gabriel was a work partner of Andy's and the good news was that Andy had decided to give me a share of one of his new businesses. So this gave me and the kids had a regular income. I tried hard to brush off her questions; luckily it was her mobile ring tone that saved the day.

"OK... I will be ten mins." Ellie's husband was quizzing her again. "I got to go, Pol... I'm sorry do you want me to order you a taxi, too?"

"Erm, no it's fine I will grab one from the rank, is everything OK?" I saw her twitching in her seat.

"Not really, Polly, you know how he controls me." Sadness filled her eyes, the fun loving Ellie quickly disappeared.

"Whatever you do, Polly... don't be with a man that calls the shots, make sure you have total control, or you will end up like me." She leaned over and kissed my cheek, gathered her stuff and hastily walked towards the door.

Feeling sad for my friend I just nodded, no questions asked I just allowed her to go. Ellie had always struggled with her bloke. She left him once and he won her back, it wasn't long before he slipped back to his old ways. He was a man of whisky, fine dining and multiple affairs, I don't think I will ever understand why men do this to beautiful caring women, maybe all men are void of the caring emotions.

I finished my drink, grabbed my bag and prepared to leave for the taxis rank. Gabriel had noticed I was lonesome, like a knight he rose to my rescue.

"Polly, are you leaving so soon?"

"Yes, Ellie's had to go home, so that's my cue." Wow he made me nervous.

"OK, at least allow me to walk you to the taxi rank."

I glanced behind him at his friend, then back at him.

"I insist!" He demanded.

This was a nice feeling someone wanting to keep me safe. I rose from my seat and followed him out of the club.

The air was cool, my body started to shiver. To my surprise Gabriel took off his jacket and placed it over my shoulders, whilst gently repositioning my curls over my back sending tingles around my whole body. We walked to the taxis rank in silence, he seemed to know a lot of people, there was a lot of hello's along the way.

He grabbed a taxi, even though we were last in the queue, even the cab driver knew his name, who the bloody hell was he? How come everyone else knows this gorgeous man but me? I was stunned.

"To Lick Penny Lane, please." Mr Summer's boomed at the taxi driver.

Gabriel got in the cab with me and still said nothing.

"Where are you taking me?" I asked bewildered.

"Wait and see." He was stern and very businesslike.

I was scared, but at the same time felt safe and excited. My unleashed kitty was purring slowly whilst licking her paws.

The cab stopped, strangely down an unlit country lane. Gabriel asked the cab driver to put it on his tab and escorted me out of the car. We stood and watched the car disappear, still no words had been spoken between us and I could hear the wind gently rattling the trees and smell the forest pine. Gabriel took hold of my arm.

"Trust me and don't move, I'm not going to hurt you. It's a surprise for you."

He carefully placed a blindfold over my face, my senses heightened, my pulse raced off the scale. I only had my ears and nose to rely upon. The scent of Mr Summers increased greatly in the midnight cool air. Amazingly, I felt safe.

He took my arm and guided me down a gravelled path, with each baby step I made I couldn't help feeling out of depth even though I was full of wonder. He came to a halt, tugged my arm and carefully helped me up a series of stone steps. One by one, I knew we were getting closer to a door of some kind. The chill of the night never approached me, my body heat radiated in anticipation.

"Not far now." Gabriel announced.

I gulped, my mouth felt dry I replied with a simple croaky 'OK'.

The sound of a key in the lock echoed around me, with a click the door opened. Gabriel guided me over the door step, still holding my arm he pulled the door shut and the click of the key locked us in. I heard him flick a switch; even though I was blind folded I knew it was a light. He turned me around and undid the blind fold.

"Wow! This place is beautiful." My mouth dropped.

"Yes, it is a beautiful place, for beautiful people." He exclaimed.

I looked at Gabriel; he must have noticed my confused look.

"There's more, come. I will show you round a couple of rooms." He yet again grabbed me, but this time he took my hand.

The hallway was huge, elegant chandeliers hung from the ceiling, there was the widest flight of gilt stairs running up the middle, huge ornate mirrors lined the walls and the floor was black marble. It all shone and glistened like Cinderella's castle. He led me through a door to our right, yet another huge solid wood door. Inside the room I felt like Lady of the Manor.

"This is amazing! Do you own this castle?" I asked eager for answers and wondering why he wanted to bring me here.

"All will be revealed in time, would you like a drink? We can talk next to the fire." He walked to the drinks bar and beckoned me to perch on a stool.

I sat gazing at the room, the first thing I noticed was the huge roaring fireplace, with deep red huge scatter cushions carefully placed in a horse shoe shape around it and a large sheep skin rug in the middle. Large canvass paintings of naked women hung on the walls and large church like candles lit the dark corners.

"What do you use this room for?" I was feeling brave.

Gabriel placed my glass of Baileys on ice in front of me, sighed yet said nothing. Our gaze was locked, it felt like he was reading my mind, he leaned over the bar and gently stroked my face with the back of his hand.

"I'm going to be direct with you, Polly."

"Please do." I felt my whole being twinge, my tigress pert her ears ready to listen.

"I want you, I want to enjoy you and I want to feel what it's like to be inside you." His face straight, still locked in my gaze.

I was dumbstruck, why would he want me? This young rich handsome man wants me… but he has a wife and family. Oh shit, what do I do? He walked round to my side of the bar, took my hand and guided me to the sofa area. He asked me to sit on the biggest sofa I had ever seen, all made in glorious deep red velvet heavily decorated in gold scatter cushions.

I sat like a good little girl obeying my Master; my once safe mode started fraying at the edges. OK, so now I'm feeling a touch uncomfortable. He just stood there staring at me. My breathing started to quicken, panic showed its ugly head, I jumped up.

"I've got to go. I need to be back… It's late!" I placed the drink which was still full on the delicate three legged table at the side of me and headed for the door.

"Stop!" Shouted Gabriel, large thudding steps echoed as he approached me.

Gabriel grabbed my arm yet again, with his body language demanding me to stand still for the Master. So yet again, I did as I was told.

"Let me explain… then I will call a cab and you can go home and think about what I've said, you will control the situation… I promise." He noticed my surprise.

I allowed him to escort me back to the seating area in front of the simmering fire. Sitting back down I felt reassured, picked my drink up and took a sip, then I just came out with it.

"So, Mr Summers… you want to have sex with me… as a business deal? Or a relationship? Because I have a problem with this… FOR GODS SAKE, YOU'RE MARRIED!"

Gabriel was still standing opposite me, smiling at me he sat next to me, keeping a slight distance between us. He raised his glass to his mouth, slowly drank a little of the Baileys, cocked his head to one side and laughed.

"DON'T LAUGH AT ME!" I screamed at him.

"Whoa… calm down, you are seriously turning me on with your little angry outbursts." He replied laughing, then he composed himself quickly as he realised I was not backing down.

"OK, I will explain. My wife and I… well, we have an open kind of relationship. To start with we had a marriage of convenience. Both our parents are stinking rich and they wanted to protect their wealth and who inherited the money when they pass away. So they got together and destined us to be married from birth, they even had it drawn up in a contract incase they died before we reached eighteen. That was when we had to get married. Our parents controlled everything, the day, date and

42

even the time. There was nothing she or I could do." Gabriel relaxed into the back of the sofa and drunk all his drink in one.

With this new revelation I eased a little; Gabriel looked at me for a response. Placing my glass on the side table, I allowed my purring Tigress to guide me. She ushered me across to Gabriel, his face was soft with the glow of the fire. I was in control, that's what he said, so being me that was my green light to apply it now.

Looking at him I gently stroked his face, my body pulsating with urge, I gently pressed my lips against his. Electrical waves flooded my body; my nipples became erect with excitement. He knew this was my answer, I didn't need to say a word, he became very responsive, but I would only allow him what I wanted after all I was in control. Gabriel gently placed his hand on my dress gently circling and stoking my nipple, I winced at the shock and took a deep breath in. He eased my straps off both my shoulders, keeping his gaze locked with mine; with both hands he gradually revealed my engorged breasts. My heart raced as he teased my erect nipples with his fingers. Circling and stroking them, I threw my head back in ecstasy as he gently twisted each one then licked his fingers and circled each one again and again. I could feel the throb in my groin, my body withered in the heat of his touch. His lips joined mine; currents ran through me as we passionately kissed by firelight. Fuelled by alcohol and adrenalin I ran my fingers through his hair allowing my nails to excite the back of his neck, he thrust onto me. I could feel his hard manhood pressing on my pubic bone, his soft moist lips kissed my aroused nipples, he trailed his tongue around them then right up to my chin before he locked his lips with mine. I could taste the liquor from his tongue as he devoured me. Then I pulled back and moved away from him. Gabriel looked puzzled; he leaned over to pull me towards him.

"I thought I was in control?" I announced trying to compose myself.

"You are." He replied in little boy voice.

"Then I would like that taxi you promised me, the quicker the better please."

"Have I upset you, Polly?" Gabriel scratched his hair into place.

"No… You haven't upset me, but I need to think… alone."

Gabriel called me a cab; he used first name terms to the lady on the phone. Both of us stood at the front door yet again, this time the taxi came to the front of the house, so why did he make me walk up the drive? I turned and looked at him. God, he was stunning and smelt even nicer than ever, but even with my need of him I knew I had to go, something just didn't add up, something was missing here, I could smell a rat. As I climbed in the taxi, Gabriel handed me a folded piece of paper.

"Read this when you get home and not until."

"OK." Was all I could say.

He closed the door, banged twice on the roof and the taxi left Lick Penny Lane.

6

Shutting my front door behind me, I collapsed my body on the back of the door in a state of shock. "What the bloody hell just happened?" Words escaped my mouth.

"Hi, Mum, I've been waiting up for you." Chloe popped up from nowhere, she looked puzzled as she realised I was alone. "Who are you talking to?" Chloe asked

My mind snapped back into the here and now. "No one, sweetie… what are you doing here? I thought you were staying with your dad?"

"Yes, I just forgot my iPod, can't live without my tunes. Where have you been? Are you OK? You look flustered?"

"I've been out with Ellie, she got summoned by that bloke of hers and I had to get a cab back on my own… but it took all night to get one, the queue was massive." Hopefully that should keep her quiet.

"Oh, I see. If I would have known I could have got Dad to pick you up on the way. He dropped me off earlier as he's got an important client to see in the morning, so he's staying at Gran's then driving down there in the morning, he's only got an hours travel. When he's done, he's picking me back up."

We both went into the living room; I sat down kicking my shoes off and started rubbing my aching feet.

"I'm going to bed now, Mum... oh and you look lovely, did you pull?" Chloe had a smirky grin on her face.

"Pull? I'm too old for that, young lady... Good Night, Chloe." Shaking my head at my daughter she just laughed, then winked at me as she headed for the stairs.

Crikey, can she tell? I stood looking in the mirror above the fireplace. A very content feline was staring back nursing her paws as she purred. I noticed I looked a little flush and my hair was messed up slightly... hold on maybe it was my bra straps. Oh dear, I'd pulled my dress straps up and forgotten my bra straps, they were just dangling either side of my dress. Hmmm must be more careful, it was obvious that Chloe noticed. Definitely time for a cup of tea, I need to calm down and collect my thoughts or my night's sleep just isn't going to happen.

I made my tea and decided to do some thinking in bed, my bedroom was my personal space, a space I so needed right now. I slumped myself on the bed; still trying to sooth my poor feet from those ridiculous shoes, like lightening it struck me... the piece of paper! Oh God, where is it? Panic set in; frantically I got up recovering my steps to find it. I went back to the kitchen, living room and front door but nothing, feeling highly disappointed I crawled back up to bed, left my clothes on and got underneath my duvet... in the small hours of the morning, I'd done something I vowed never to do again... I cried myself to sleep.

Chloe woke me with a hot English brew. She placed it on my bedside table and sat on the edge of my bed. Her face was sullen, there was obviously something wrong, I smiled at her sat up and gave her a hug.

"Chloe, thanks for the tea, what's wrong, hunny?" Pulling back, I waited for her reply.

"Nothing, Mum... I'm OK, did you sleep well?" I could tell by her tone of voice she was lying.

She got up and opened my curtains to let the sunlight in, it was blinding and all I could see was tiny dust particles swirling around the room. Chloe looked beautiful as ever, even if she was still in her PJ's and slippers.

"See you downstairs, Mum. Dad's picking me up at 3pm." Chloe left my room.

I checked my watch, it was twelve noon- blimey, I better get a move on. I jumped in the shower, scrubbed every inch of my body, eradicating Gabriel Summers' finger prints from my skin. I washed my hair a dozen times to get the smell of his aftershave off me, never again would I allow this man to lure me in, even if I did feel a connection, he was STILL married and trying invade my life and at my age I should know better than to trust a man I barely knew. So today is a fresh day, I will greet Chloe with a smile and carry on as normal.

It was quarter past two. Chloe had prepared herself for her dad's return. She seemed to find more stuff to take with her and amazingly left a huge pile of hers and Josh's washing behind. She was wearing her normal attire of jeans, t-shirt and red Converse; she'd tied her hair into a side pony tail and was wearing more make up than normal. Remembering Chloe's sad moment on my bed, I decided to dig a little.

"You look nice, Chloe."

"Thanks." She replied, rummaging through her bags.

OK, so she seems fine.

"Have you made any new friends whilst you've been at Dad's?"

"Yes, a few!"

One word answers from Chloe weren't helping.

"Chloe," I grabbed her for a hug, "if you ever need to talk to me about anything... anything at all, I'm here... you know that, don't you?"

"Mum, I will be fine... it's just... " There was a knock at the door.

Thinking it was her dad, even though it was earlier than 3pm, I sent Chloe to the door. I sat at the kitchen table, cupping my warm tea, trying my hardest not to listen in on their conversation. Strangely, that didn't happen. Chloe shut the door after saying 'Thank you' to whoever it was on my door step.

"It's for you, Mum... what is it?" Chloe was intrigued.

She handed me a white sealed envelope and sat down opposite me at the table.

"It looks to me like it's a white envelope."

"Yes, I can see that, but what's in it?"

"How am I supposed to know? Who was at the door?"

"It was a taxi man. He said you left this in his car last night." Chloe's eyes widened some more.

I drank my tea, unable to answer her questions; if I ever wanted her dad to come it was right now. Someone upstairs must have heard me; there was another knock at the door.

"Your dad's here... come on, don't keep him waiting." I jumped up to help her.

"Come on, Mum, open it... what is it?" She stood in the doorway tilting her head at me.

"I will ring you later, your dad's waiting... CHLOE!" My temper was beginning to fray.

"OK, keep your hair on! Love ya, Mum." She kissed me and left.

I shut the door and hurried to the kitchen. I made another cup of tea and sat at my table looking at the letter which I had propped up against the fruit bowl. An hour had passed and I was still mesmerised by the letter, knowing deep down it contained the piece of paper that Gabriel gave me last night. I was testing my will and curiosity and was wondering if I was actually strong enough... or would I crumble and tear the damn thing open? I decided on a hot bubble bath, so I could think some more. I wasn't one for decisions and this one was churning my stomach inside out.

I placed my slippers and dressing gown on the radiator, even though it was warm outside I always liked a warm set of clothes to change into.

As the bath was running my mobile went off, it was Ellie.

"Hi, Ellie!"

"Hi, hun, did you get home OK last night?" Ellie's voice was quiet.

"Yes, I got a taxi. Was that prick of a man of yours OK with you?" I was harsh.

"Yeah, he sulked a bit like normal, he's given me the silent treatment most of the day and now he's just announced he's going out tonight and staying at his mates house!" Her voice was shaky.

"Oh my God!! He's got some nerve, whose house he staying at?"

"I don't know, he told me his name is Mark and he works with him… I'm going to be on my own, so I wondered if you fancy going out for a drink or a meal?"

Ellie's voice was clearly desperate, I could tell she was thinking the worst; he always was a player and a control freak.

"Can do, what time shall I be ready?"

"8pm OK? He will be gone by then, so I can get ready without him knowing."

"OK… see you later, are you coming to mine first?"

"Yeah, I will leave my car at yours, see you later, you're a diamond, Polly."

She hung up, obviously arranging tonight in secret, our conversation was rushed.

I sunk into my bath, at least I would be squeaky clean for tonight, my thoughts turned to what I was going to wear, knowing Ellie it would be a meal and drinks. When her fella is not around she makes her evenings out well worth it. In my head I pictured wearing a tight red dress with black diamanté evening shoes and wearing my hair down with a silver diamanté head band. Maybe that was too over dressed for a meal and a few drinks, I reached for my phone and text Ellie and if I knew what she was wearing I would have some indication of what to wear myself. I stood my phone up in the bathroom window waiting on Ellie's reply when my eye caught sight of my strange envelope which was propped on the soap basket on the sill.

Putting on my warm dressing gown and slippers I reached for the envelope. With apprehension, I carefully tore the envelope open. With a deep breath I pulled out the letter. My first instinct was to burn the damn thing and erase all memories of the night before, my second instinct was to leave it until after my night out with Ellie, but my final instinct was to open it up and feed my curiosity of what the wonderful Mr Summers had given me. I unfolded the letter, the first thing I noticed was the golden letter header 'Summer's Golden Entertainment' across the top in old italic with red roses sat amongst the letters. I read further.

Dear Polly Perkins,

We would like to invite you to our Halloween Ball on the 31st of October 2013 at 8pm at Golden Gates Club. Dress standards apply, on arrival you will be given a fancy dress costume to change into. To gain entry you will present your letter to our doorman along with your personal password, this will be sent out to you in due course. This event is of high security, under no circumstances do you disclose any information of this party to anyone, anyone who isn't on the list will be turned away and anyone who brings a guest will be asked to leave and shall be disqualified from future events. We hope you treat this in high confidentiality and we look forward to seeing you there.

Many thanks
Mr & Mrs Summers
Summers Golden Entertainment

Feeling slightly disappointed I lay on my bed to think, a party invite to that house... not sure I want to go back there... or do I? And it's signed from him and his wife, why would he want me to go? His wife will be there and what's with all this security stuff? Surely that's not necessary...

or is it? It sounds quite formal so what's the big secret? Hmm password, according to this I can't tell anyone neither, so telling Ellie is out of the question. And there's me thinking it would have been a love letter, or an apology or a phone number, how wrong I was then. I can't even tell Chloe and I know she will ask me later today, I need to sit and think about this... but I really want to find out more. Do I... or don't I? Time for a cup of tea and time to make another list.

7

It was quite warm for an early October morning. Josh had given me the parents evening letter, late as usual. This was the first time I would be face to face with his father since August. I stayed hidden for the most of last month, trying to compose myself from Gabriel Summers and his bloody country house. Ellie had been 'grounded' by her controlling husband, so our only connection was sneaky phone calls and emails. Chloe had landed herself a boyfriend from where her dad lives, so she wasn't around much at weekends. It just became me and Josh, unless he was at his dad's, Gran's or at friend's sleep over. The only thing that kept my spirits up was my internet dating. Even though most of my replies for my advert were quite disgusting, it did make me chuckle. One of the contacts I have was allowed the honour of my mobile number, but we have yet to meet up. After Mr Summers, I'm definitely taking my time.

I walked with Josh to the main gates of his school. Josh was in his designer gear and hi-tops, I had found my woollen black knee length dress, accompanied with my long black leather boots a bright purple belt and silk scarf to match. The wonderful 'HIM' should be impressed, I'm not brown anymore and I'm now black.

"Josh... Josh!"

"Oh hi, Dad." Josh looked at me.

There in front of me was Andrew and his new squeeze! This was the first time I had the pleasure of meeting her. I stood back and allowed Josh to greet his dad and 'her'. She was dainty and overly bleached blonde. She wore a salmon, figure hugging dress with grey high heels. Her skin was sun bed brown and she wore red, 'in your face' lipstick. She smiled at me with a perfect set of bleached teeth. I just nodded with a slow smile of politeness. I can see why he fell for her; she's one of those annoying 'perfect' women that most of us avoid. I glanced at her hands, the ring on her finger was a statement of 'he's my husband now'. She wore a huge emerald engagement ring.

He must have spent a fortune. So much for my first engagement ring; it was a plastic ring from an egg out of a fairground machine. He knew I always wanted a real one. A year later, whilst I was pregnant, he bought me an extremely small diamond ring in sterling silver. I think my pregnancy hormones helped me get that, but I never did get the wedding band I so desired. I obviously (judging by his new wife) wasn't his type at all.

I walked with Josh in to the main hall; the school was beautiful and also very old. It used to be an all boys school in the 1700's. The flooring was parquet wood, the walls were covered in wooden panels painted cream. A large picture gallery of all the pervious headmasters hung above an old, disused fireplace. You could feel their eyes following you, or maybe that was Andrew's wife watching my every move.

The Head Master and a few teachers stood chatting in a huddle at the front of room. Chairs were lined in rows and faced towards the small gathering of teachers. The front row of seats where filled by a small number of eager parents, quietly talking amongst themselves about their children.

Andrew chose the row and seats, his bride sat next to him with Josh next, then me. That left two seats on my side next to the centre aisle. It was only a few minutes before the hall filled up nicely. An elegant lady around my age sat next to me and placed her Louis Vuitton handbag on the other chair. She obviously had an air of wealth around her; her perfume and style of dress was bordering on aristocracy. Wonder filled my mind. Who has she saved the seat for? I wonder what her husband (she had a wedding ring) looks like. Images of lords and ladies flashed at me, sophisticated dinner party's with waiters pouring wine from crystal decanters. Huge long oak tables set with silver table wear, with shiny candelabra's placed in the middle amongst the fabulous smelling roasts and steaming fresh vegetables.

"Hello, I'm Grace; I don't think we've met before."

"Oh, hello, I'm Polly. No I don't think we have." The Lady of the Manor caught me checking her out.

"Is your child doing well here?" Knowing that was a crap question, I grimaced inside.

"Oh no, I haven't got any children here, they're too young yet. I'm the Governess of the school."

"Oh I see, I'm sorry I didn't realise. Nice to meet you." Hoping that was a better response, I smiled at her and made a quick getaway to the ladies in embarrassment.

I didn't quite make the toilets as my mobile went off. I took the phone call outside the school; it was only Ellie on one of her sneaky phone moments. At least it gave me time to get over my 'feeling stupid and intimidated moment'. I must work on my confidence issues, first Andrew's wife and then someone whom I've never met!

Quickly, I dashed to the girls bathroom, at that moment a familiar smell caught my attention. The hairs on my arms stood up, my heart began to beat at speed and the air surrounding me was intoxicating. Feeling too scared to turn round I froze. His warm breath fell on my neck as he whispered words of excitement in my ear, but I refused to turn around, in fact I was unable to turn to face him. I had completely put Mr

54

Summers out of my head; well, I thought I had, judging by my body's response, maybe not!

I waited until his footsteps echoed down the hall before I moved from my spot outside the toilets. I headed straight for the sinks, my face was ashen, my fingers shaky. Damn this man! Why does he have this effect on me? Am I really that weak? I splashed water on my face; my reflection was a sliding mess of make-up. As I touched up my face, to make myself a little more presentable, Andrew's new squeeze walked in. I really couldn't be bothered with this now, so I just managed an 'Oh God it's you!' smile and left to join Josh.

Unfortunately, I had missed the whole talk, Josh didn't seem bothered when I told him. I felt a bit sick and I was stuck in the bathroom. Little did he know his mother was a wimp, even the new look doesn't change the person inside. I need to find my tigress, the one that kept my spirits up. She had left me since Gabriel Summers had been put on the 'Dangerous' shelf in my mind, maybe I had left her there with him.

I needed to escape and fast. Josh told his dad I felt unwell so Andrew agreed to accompany him to speak with his form tutor. Josh walked off in front with his dad by his side and the little 'wifey' began trotting closely behind them trying to keep up.

I barely got out of the school car park when I received a text on my mobile.

'All I can say is, you look beautiful, Polly xx' I couldn't believe my eyes. It was Andrew's mobile!

This is too overwhelming for me, my ex-partner who thought I was a mess gives me a compliment and Gabriel Summers in Josh's school. Why was he there? And those words he spoke softly in my ear, "I want you Polly," and having to cope with Andrew's wife and who was that intimidating woman who sat next to me? I needed Ellie, but what can I tell her? I didn't do anything; I just went home and put the kettle on.

As I sat at the kitchen table cupping my drink, I began to feel a lot better and relaxed. Thoughts of the evening refused to leave my mind. I tried reading and watching soaps. I even ran a bath but nothing worked. It wouldn't be long until Josh was home; I needed to get my thoughts back to normal so Josh couldn't quiz my absent mindedness. That's when Ellie rang.

"Polly?" Her voice was weak.

"Ellie, are you OK?"

"No, Polly can I come and stay with you for a couple of days?" Now she sounded desperate.

"Of course you can. Ellie, what's happened? Are you OK?" I realised that was a really stupid question.

"I will explain when I get to your house; it's that husband of mine. I will be ten minutes."

"OK, just come straight in Ellie."

"Will do, thank you, Polly, you're a star." She put the phone down.

I was quite worried, Ellie's husband was a tricky one. The last thing I wanted was this big, burly man to come and bang my door down. So this meant I had Josh and Ellie due at the same time. Even though I didn't want to, I had to inform Andrew, maybe he could take Josh somewhere for an hour until I sorted Ellie out. I really didn't want to, especially after the last text he sent me. Do I thank him for the compliment or ignore it? Why does my mind have to be so complicated? I decided to flip a penny; heads was to thank him, tails to ignore his comment. It came up tails.

Ellie walked in and collapsed sobbing in my arms. She was unable to speak so I guided her to the sofa and placed a brew in her hands with a man size box of tissues. After twenty minutes or so she calmed down.

"Polly, thank you for letting me crash here tonight."

"You're welcome; you can stop with me any time you want. Ellie, what's happened?"

"He's got another woman." The sobs started again.

So now I'm getting angry, what is it with today's men? They seem to hurt and push a woman's trust to the limit. Surely there must be a good kind hearted man out there who will love you until your dying day. All this doesn't help women, we are creatures of love, comfort and stability and I for one still want a companion. So like all the other girls out there, we still keep trying.

I managed to get Ellie in the bath so I could tell Josh why she was here and that her husband had been a naughty boy. Josh laughed and said it was only a matter of time. He was right but also callous for laughing at my best friend's dilemma. Josh proceeded to tell me how Ellie's husband had been talking to Andrew a lot recently, so that explains it. He's another one that has gone for a younger model, obviously thinking the grass is greener. Money and power... but wait a minute, I also have money. Time to create my own power and I'm going to give some to Ellie, too. This will be fun.

8

Ellie had been with us for two weeks now. She and Jack had officially split up but he had left her homeless and penniless. It amazed me how he was the one in the wrong, but he retained everything, as they didn't have any children together. Ellie couldn't have children, but she always had open arms for his twin boys; they went to stay with them every other weekend.

Jack had no idea I had a large, nice nest egg, split in to three different bank accounts. Even Ellie didn't know how much I had stashed away; in fact no one did, only me. Now Ellie was living here I had to be careful with my paper work, apart from one piece of paper, that I deliberately left on my bedroom dresser.

Chloe was sharing her room with Ellie, but as Chloe wasn't here that much they never clashed. Chloe had decided to work for her dad and dump the idea of going to college; to me it was a planned mission she even lives with him ninety percent of the week. I knew it was because her boyfriend lived that way. She never did tell me properly, she sort of just slipped in to the job bit by bit. Maybe it was her way of easing me in to her new life. London was now her first home.

Ellie was wonderful at first; she had no job so on my working days she cleaned the house for me, top to bottom. The washing was always done, ironed, folded and even put away. She kept me company as the nights turned darker and even cooked a lovely Sunday roast for my mum and dad on one of their weekly visits. This didn't last long; Ellie slipped in to depression. Soon she struggled to get up in the mornings, left dirty laundry everywhere, failed to wash a single pot and most of all she took up my favourite chair in the living room.

We needed a chat, emotionally she was struggling and physically so was I. Even Josh who had known her for the last ten years refused to be in the same room as her. The fun loving, bouncy Ellie had slipped away along with her marriage. Jack may have controlled her, but he obviously kept her in line and sane, with me she had to rediscover herself and find out who she was and what she wanted in life.

I organised the chat wisely, leaving Josh at my mother's for the weekend giving us the time and space to find where the real Ellie had gone. It was a Friday night; I knew she wouldn't be up for a night out like she did to me when I split with Andrew, so I organized a little party. I invited a few work friends, who were all male apart from one and a couple of mothers from Josh's school.

Ellie went for a bath as I spruced the house and lay nibbles and cocktail glasses out on the kitchen table. Ellie had lost so much weight, so none of her clothes fit her. I helped her find something to wear out of Chloe's left overs and then I jumped in the shower to replenish my energy levels.

I decided to dress casually, choosing a pair of black linen trousers and a red, tight strappy top. The cottage warms up really well, especially with a few more bodies knocking around. Ellie however had decided on Chloe's black cat suit. It fit her perfectly; being strapless it showed off her delicate shoulders. She put her hair in a high bun, accentuating her neck; she looked amazing. I'm so glad she made the effort; I just hope she smiles a little bit.

My guests started to arrive; George came first loaded with Pimm's, several bottles of lemonade and a couple of bags of fresh mint.

"Hi, Polly."

"Hi, George, do come in." George hugged me tight and then he spotted Ellie.

"Well, hello, who's this?" He asked, holding his hand out to Ellie's.

"George, meet Ellie, my best friend." George took Ellie's hand and planted a soft kiss upon it.

Ellie blushed, but more importantly she smiled and boy it was a big one.

I left the two of them to get to know each other as there was a knock at the door again. Thomas, Giles and Stephanie greeted me with a bottle of Martini Bianco and a bag full of fruit. Stephanie, to my delight had also bought some after dinner mints, a chocolate orange, spray cream and a small bottle of brandy. The cocktails were going to be varied tonight, with lots of different ingredients we were all in for a good tasting session.

Ellie and George were getting on like a house on fire. I soon realised she craved male attention and needed it to keep her low self esteem on a high. A few more guests arrived making it a total of ten of us. The cottage was full of laughter now and the cocktails were flowing nicely too, that's when I decided to get the games out.

"Cluedo or Monopoly?" I asked my tipsy, giggly friends.

We ended up on a voting system, Cluedo won by majority. We played the game which ended with Emma (one of the mum's from school) correctly guessing the answer, which was Professor Plum in the kitchen with the lead piping. As Emma won she got to choose the next game. This game however Ellie and George decided to sit out.

George has always been a lovely bloke; we got on like brother and sister. Many times George would pop round to mine in my bleak days after Andrew left me. I'd always thought he was a bit on the gay side, until tonight seeing him with Ellie, this showed me a different side to him.

It was a good hour before I realised they had both disappeared from downstairs. I wasn't overly concerned, George being thirty eight and Ellie being thirty five; they were old enough to choose their own path of delights. I was just glad that Ellie was finding herself again.

The party soon came to a close; I hugged each guest in turn as they left for their journey home. Only George was left. I tidied up the rooms, keeping hold of the booze that was unopened, just in case there was another party lurking around the corner.

As I plumped the cushions on the sofa, my hand caught on something hard, it was my mobile. Five missed calls and two new messages: two calls from Andrew, one call from my new friend off the internet and two calls from the same number, but this person was not on my friends list. I checked out my texts. One from Josh, saying 'Night, Mum' and the other was from the mystery number which called twice. 'Meet me at midnight, PLEASE, Polly and don't be late, outside the Kings Arms. Tell no one. GS.'

Oh no, how did he get my number? My watch said eleven thirty; I had half an hour to decide what to do. It's pretty dark; I would be on my own, I must be mad to even consider it. I made a drink of tea, sat at the kitchen table in total shock of my phone. First I thought I had better call Andrew back to check what he wanted. That's when I noticed an answer phone message. I dialled the number, it was Andrew.

"Hi Pol, I was just giving you a quick call to see if you're free Sunday night this week? I've got something for Josh and I'm seeing my mum so I was going to pop over for a cup of tea and a chat. It was lovely to see you the other week, you look really well, speak soon." I pressed delete; he's got some bloody cheek. I wonder why he's creeping so much. I must make sure Ellie stays with me; I don't trust 'HIM'.

My thoughts returned to my mystery text. What the hell, Ellie seems happy with George, I'll leave a note. I picked up my pepper spray, better to be safe than sorry. I collected a few things; money, mobile phone, spare house keys and mini torch.

All that was left was a quick wash and a squirt of perfume. I gently pulled the door shut so not to alert my house mate and her new found friend.

The moon was full, giving me extra light as I walked towards the pub. My breath hung in the crisp air, my nose stung with the cold. It wasn't far to the Kings Arms. I felt strangely at ease with the fact that he had my mobile number, not so happy at the fact that he was so close to my home, which means he must know where I live. Frost was beginning to set under foot so I trod very carefully, with each step I crunched the ground, using all my concentration to stay upright. I approached my destination more quickly than I expected, which surprised me as I'd had quite a few cocktails this evening.

OK, so I'm on my own and he's not here. I looked at my watch. It was five minutes to midnight. I knew that if he was not here soon, then I wouldn't be either. It was late, dark and cold. Midnight approached, I checked my mobile, nothing. At five past midnight I gave up. Mad at myself for believing he would be here, my pace quickened. Then it occurred to me, it might not have been him! Now I felt stupid again and hurt. I sent a quick text to the unknown number.

'Screw you!' I pressed send.

I stood under the only street light on the lane, waiting for a reply. My mobile vibrated.

'I'm behind you and yes please.'

I spun round and there he was smiling like nothing had happened. Oh this man winds me up!

"Hello, Polly, would you like a lift in my car?" He held out his hand.

"Hello, Gabriel." I replied through gritted teeth.

Yet again no words were spoken in the taxi. The driver took us to the same house as before. I squirmed as we sat together on the back seat. Gabriel looked alluring, dressed in a long black over coat and his smell

62

engulfed all my senses. We got out of the taxi; he grabbed my hand and led me down the path towards the front door. He stopped, turned to face me and very gently stroked the side of my face.

"You're very beautiful, Polly. Don't worry, all I want tonight is your company. I've not stopped thinking about you, but Polly, I still want you." He fumbled with the key in the lock and escorted me in.

Gabriel took me a different way than before. This room was towards the back of the house, he switched each individual light off as we went. Inside, the walls were tiled, the floor to match. The room was steamy and in the centre was the biggest wooden hot tub I had ever seen. The lights changed colour from yellow to green to red then blue. Green palm trees lined the corners, with glittering mirrors fitted to the ceiling. Large golden towel rails were sporting fluffy white towels and to the side of the hot tub was a small wooden beach bar with a bottle of champagne on ice.

"Wow! This looks amazing." I was dumbfounded.

"Yes, it's quite something. The water's bubbling nicely, the temperature is just right. I will leave you to it, Polly. Enjoy yourself in my tub. I will be back in five minutes to join you." He kissed me on the cheek then left.

9

I slipped my clothes off as quickly as possible, checking the door constantly, the last thing I needed was Gabriel catching me half naked bent over with my ass hanging out. I hung my trousers, top and underwear on the pegs provided and gently eased my right leg in to the hot bubbles. When I was fully immersed in the soothing water I lay my head back and gazed up at the mirrored ceiling. And there I was; naked, chilled and very relaxed. The alcohol definitely helped me get here; I wouldn't have the courage without it.

Ten minutes must have passed before Gabriel walked through the door. He looked lush; his body was provocatively wrapped in a fluffy white towel. His skin was beautifully tanned with just enough chest hair that I could run my fingers through. I so wanted to devour him, to taste his bodily flavour and take him for my own. I melted in his everlasting gaze, hoping there was space in there for me.

"Would you like a drink, Polly?" His voice was deep and smooth.

"Yes, thank you." Was all I could manage.

He poured the champagne in to the flutes from the bar area and popped a strawberry in each glass. He oozed confidence, I could tell he was enjoying watching me twist my hair round my fingers, he smiled and handed me the glass.

"Is it OK to join you, Mrs Perkins?" He leaned over the back of me, blatantly staring at my submerged breasts.

"Please, be my guest."

He kissed the top of my head and walked around to the front of the tub. He paused, smiled then unwrapped his towel and laid it on the floor. Wow! And there he stood, completely naked and totally comfortable with it. I couldn't help but look. His body looked inviting; I quickly ran my eyes over his chest down to his perfectly formed weapon. It just hung there. My body tingled, as my mind envisioned me to feel through his dark curly hair and tease the length of his soft manhood whilst watching tentatively at his growing arousal.

He must have noticed my private amusement; his arousal began to show.

"OK, I know what you're doing… stop it." He entered the water to break the connection.

Gabriel moved around to my side brushing my warm skin as he approached. My skin fizzed at his touch and the bubbles made my feelings last longer transferring prickles all over me.

"Polly… can we talk?" He leaned towards me, his eyes locked with mine.

"Of course, what would you like to chat about?"

"You, I need to know more about you."

"Well, there's not much to know… but I have a few questions." Oh God I didn't want to talk, not now any way.

"OK how about, you ask me a question and then I will ask you a question. Is that fair?"

I looked at him, not quite what I had in mind right now, but this subject needed dealing with so I can have my wicked way with him. My body deflated, my need outweighed my speech, so I just gave him a nod.

"OK, fire away."

65

I'm sure he was enjoying watching me squirm, I felt vulnerable yet hungry for him at the same time, so I decided to be direct, hoping this would be over quickly.

A thousand questions came to mind, but as I wanted to concentrate on his body, I couldn't think of one that would cover them all. I drank the champagne, placed the glass down on the edge of the hot tub, took a deep breath then just came out with the most obvious one.

"Why me?" Hoping I wasn't sounding too desperate.

He instantly knew what I meant by that and was quick to answer.

"Polly, I like you. You're a lot older than the women I normally go for but, you're beautiful, sexy and intelligent. I feel this wonderful connection between us and you make me feel comfortable and nervous at the same time. I'm drawn to you."

I was aghast! He finds me beautiful and sexy, I can agree with the intelligent bit but I'm naive for my age. In fact I would say I'm bordering on stupid. The connection, it's nice to know he feels it too, my gut instinct is obviously working properly again but this bloke has ties, one being his wife!

"Why are you still married? And what does your wife think about your behaviour?" My words just blurted out; even if it was his turn I had to understand the truth.

He frowned, "Polly, that's two questions and you've not allowed me to ask you mine yet!"

Moments of silence passed between us, I could tell I had to play fair with him, I felt like a naughty school girl. He looked annoyed; he moved his body to the other side of me, gently brushing my nipples with his hands, blatantly doing this on purpose. My nipples became erect and my throbbing need grew to new heights. Gabriel refilled our glasses with a cheeky grin etched on his face. This was all a game to him; he was persecuting me for the second question.

"Polly, my wife is only my wife through circumstances. We were told by our families that we were to be married at a young age. She too has relations outside the family home, we're only friends but have to pretend that we're a proper couple in front of our families. The reasons for this I can't tell you. She knows I'm here with you. My life with her is a carved out plan and I love my children, they are the best thing to come from all this. If you come to our Halloween party, you will get to meet her and there you will see for yourself our real relationship as man and wife."

Wow, I wasn't expecting that! And with that he must have known he'd answered two of my questions in one. With his answer I have new questions, but I felt this wasn't the time or place to question him further on this subject.

The hot water bubbled away, I was getting very tipsy on the endless supply of alcohol that Gabriel was giving me and my body ached for his and my mind started racing. I was experiencing far too many emotions for a woman of my age, who just wants a simple comfortable life. That's when I realised this man would take me out of my comfort zone and unleash my dark hidden side.

"Right, it's my turn." Gabriel came closer to me, my heart pounded with anticipation.

"Polly, what do you want for your future?"

Shocked at his question I choked on my drink. OK, so now I was slightly scared. This question is like my lists, even though I had them I didn't quite know what I did want, or need apart from Gabriel to make love to me. I started living from day to day, always one step at a time. That's when it hit me.

"I don't know." Knowing that wouldn't be enough for him.

"You must have something in mind, Polly; after all you're the wealthiest woman I've been naked with." He smiled.

Oh God! I forgot about the money and with what he just said I realised only Gabriel knows exactly how rich I am right now. Maybe that's why he wants me so much. My mood changed. If he wants plans he's going to get them, after all I've always been a good story teller and after this I'm going home for a cup of tea.

"Gabriel, I've got plans," I sat straight conforming myself, "With my new found wealth, I will be starting up a new business in the next month. I've spoken to my financial advisor and he informs me I have plenty of money for my new venture without losing any interest for my every day costs." I paused, I'm going to have to tell him what it is, "With due respect, I can't disclose any information at the moment until all discussions and deals have been finalised. So does that answer your question, Gabriel? And if it does could I please get a lift home now, I've got a big day with work tomorrow."

He was very quiet, my tigress wanted to play. I kissed him gently on the cheek and got out of the hot tub, I couldn't believe I was doing this. There in front of him, I stood stark bollock naked and for the first time in my life I didn't care what he, or anyone, thought. His mouth dropped open when I turned around to face him. I gently eased the white fluffy robe over my body leaving my breasts and pubic region half on show. I moved my hair so it covered one of my breasts and headed for my clothes. I heard Gabriel getting out of the water; I refused to turn round to face him. He stood behind me and slowly wrapped his arms around my new confident body, gently cupping my breasts. My nipples hardened, my breathing quickened and my body arched wanting more. He groaned in my ear sending shivers down my back. My body was willing to give in but my mind was stuck in his little game. I took a step away from him and turned to face him. I had to be strong.

"I need to go home now, I have guests." I grabbed my clothes and headed for the cubicle, in a desperate need to regain my breath.

His driver dropped me in the same spot he picked me up. As I got out of the car the man handed me a letter, another one addressed to me. It was clear that this man would not give up. That rattled me, as I knew I would fall for him in a big way and I also realised I could never have a future with this man, boy he made me angry. I could have had sex with him there and then but I chose not to. I'm a lot stronger than I once thought. I needed a plan; if I was going to engage with this man then I also needed a life away from him. He has a wife, which means I need a regular boyfriend too. My life is about to get a lot more complicated and I think I kind of like it.

I ran home, I was desperate for my favourite tipple, a strong cup of tea. I opened the door quietly so not to disturb my guests, but there in front of me was Ellie with her arms folded and very messy hair. I just smiled at her new look and went for the kitchen. She followed me, leant on the door frame, squinted a bit then turned round and went back to bed. Ellie knew I wasn't going to tell her there and then, it was her way of letting me know that SHE knew I was up to something and that something, she needed to know about.

10

After Ellie and her new delight left, I decided to recap all my lists. I lay them out on the kitchen table, going through them one by one. I quickly realised that I had fulfilled most of my challenges, but somehow some of them had been mixed up, with what I wanted and what I've actually done. My thoughts returned to last night's strange events and what I had gotten myself in to, I found myself uncontrollably smiling at my strength and confidence with regards to Mr Summers.

I began writing a new list for my future.

1. Quit my job and start my new enterprise (find a business).
2. Move house (I love my house but need a change).
3. Book a holiday for me and the kids.
4. Buy a new car.
5. Take up a sport (gyms still scare me).
6. Have a massage once a week.
7. Date a new guy (to get Summers out of my head).
8. Play Summers at his own game.
9. Don't fall in love with Summers.
10. Decide whether to go to his and his wife's party.

I looked at my list, wow! It's mainly about Gabriel Summers. I decided to leave it as it is, it looks like I'm on a mission to prove myself and finally accept I have money. It's time to enjoy my life for the better.

After writing out my resignation, I put the radio on full blast and jumped in the shower to freshen up. I only had three days until Gabriel's party, so number 10 on my list was one of the first things to tackle.

I found the invite, read it over and over again. Curiosity got hold of me and my inner tigress nodded at me with her approval. "So that's that then, I'm going to his bloody party!" I was stood at my full length mirror, hands on my hips, looking very displeased with my decision. But deep down inside, I knew I had to go.

I handed in my resignation at work around lunch time. George and Steph spotted me leaving the office door.

"Hey, Polly!" Shouted George.

Shit, he clocked me; I desperately didn't want confrontation today.

"Hi, George." I shouted from a distance and carried on walking.

"Polly, hold up." Demanded Stephanie from across the shop.

George and Steph came to me; I just stood still, really not wanting this conversation right now.

"Pol... Where did you go last night? Steph's arms were crossed.

"Yeah, what happened to you? Sorry, I told Stephanie." George pursed his lips.

"OK, I met someone; it's not a crime is it?" I was not amused.

"No, but Ellie was worried about you. We came down for a cup of tea and you had gone!"

"I left you a note." I wanted to run and hide.

"Yes, I know but Ellie tried to call you and your mobile was off. If anything was to happen to you, we wouldn't know where you were or who you were with. Polly, Ellie waited up for you."

OK, so maybe George was right, but I'm forty! Surely I can look after myself. Or can I? George had real concern in his face. That explains why

Ellie didn't say much to me this morning and just got George to take her to the shopping centre before he started work.

"Look, I'm sorry guys, why don't we go out for a meal next weekend, I will pay." Blimey, I'm spending some money!

"OK." They said in unison, Steph hugged me so I said my goodbyes.

I didn't even get to tell them I wasn't going back to work, oh well, they will find out soon enough.

I arrived home with a local property paper, two massive cream cakes and a box of chocolates for Ellie. Ellie was living with me, when all along I could buy her a house out right, so the paper was for her. I found my mobile to send her a text to tell her the good news only I had to be careful what I said to her about the money. It's not that I didn't trust her, I don't trust myself, as I'm a sucker for a sob story, so the fewer people who know about the money, the better.

Five missed calls and eight text messages on my mobile. Oh God, it looks like everyone knew I had snuck out last night. This is going to take some explaining. I went through the list in order sent. Ellie had called me three times, George once and Stephanie once. My text messages however came from Ellie and Stephanie asking if I'm OK, one from Josh and one from Chloe to say their dad was coming over tonight (I forgot about HIM!), one from the guy I'm chatting with at the moment. Andrew had text me himself to check it was OK for him to pop round (so he wants something) and two from Mr Summers!

'Polly, please let me know you're home safely. GS.'

'Polly, can you text me back? And if you don't, I'm going to keep you next time I see you. GS.'

His text shocked me the most. I swiftly replied to everyone apart from GS (as he calls himself). I had to ignore him, today was not the day for mixed emotions when I had Andrew to contend with later.

Two hours later, the cottage sparkled from my cleaning, the fire crackled in the living room and the swirl of incense hung sweetly in the air. I lit perfumed candles and lay snacks on the coffee table for later. After a quick change of clothes, I popped the kettle on, knowing Ellie would be back soon.

"Hi, I'm home." Ellie burst through the door over loaded with bags.

"Wow, you've cleaned up! It looks and smells lovely, Polly." She dumped her bags on the floor.

I sat for half an hour viewing all Ellie's new purchases, wondering where she had got all this money from.

"Before you ask, George gave me some money for shopping, he's such a sweetie."

"George did? I didn't know he was so generous, Ellie."

"He offered, he said a beautiful girl like me needed spoiling." She smiled.

"So are you going to see him again, or just fleece him?"

"Polly! I would never do that to George, we're going out for a meal tonight... remember."

"But Andrew's coming round, I was banking on you to help me." I now felt crap.

"You don't need me, Polly. Chloe and Josh will be here."

She was right; I had to cope with this evening on my own even if I didn't want to. I put off the house thing for Ellie until tomorrow and just gave her the chocolates, a cup of tea and one of the huge cream cakes. Ellie was bouncy again, full of enthusiasm for life, George definitely has lifted her spirits and I was glad she didn't ask me anything about last night.

Chloe and Josh greeted me with tight hugs and kisses and as teenagers do, they both dumped their bags in the middle of the floor then raided the fridge before sitting in front of the television. Andrew just stood at the door.

"Come in then, don't just stand there!" I ushered him in, the air outside was cold.

This was the first time he had been back in the cottage since he left me for HER. I did feel a little awkward and I could tell he felt even worse. He took his coat and shoes off (one of my rules) and entered the living room.

"It looks lovely in here, Polly." He looked amazed.

"I've decorated right through, it's all different." I boasted.

I handed him a cup of tea and the chocolate digestives.

"I don't eat biscuits anymore, Leanne (his new wife) put me on a healthy eating régime," He shuffled a bit then quickly changed the subject. "So how are you, Polly?" Both kids shot him a glance.

Since we've been divorced 'HE' hasn't once asked me if I'm OK, this is very strange, first the flattering text message, then the 'Can I pop round' text and now he wants to know if I'm OK? Weird man!

I took the biscuits back, answering from the kitchen so I didn't have to face him. When I came back to the living room Andrew had successfully perched his behind in my favourite chair. This annoyed me; I would have overlooked this when I was besotted with him, but now he annoyed me.

I sat on the sofa next to the kids; I really had no idea what he was doing here or why and I wished he would hurry up so I can have a relaxing evening with my children. Chloe must have sensed my irritable mood. She got her mobile out and over her shoulder I saw she text her dad telling him to actually say something to me.

Andrew looked at his phone, cleared his throat then spoke.

"Polly, I've got something for Josh, Josh asked me to ask you if he could have it, but I need your approval first."

"OK, but first you have to tell me what it is." I didn't like the sound of this.

Josh twisted round to face me and his dad, he was eager for his dad to ask me.

"Josh wants to know if I'm allowed to buy him a motorbike for Christmas."

"Oh my God, Josh! You know my thoughts on this issue." I was not happy.

"But Mum, pleeaasse." He begged with puppy eyes.

Josh had been asking for a motor bike for years. I refused to allow him to have one as my elder brother got killed at eighteen riding a bike. It tore my heart apart; he was my big bro and my best friend.

"I can't believe you've even asked, Andrew you know how this makes me feel." I crossed my arms in disgust.

"Look, Josh and I have spoken about it at great length, I will send him on proper lessons and he can use it at my end on our land until he's seventeen, then he can take his bike test. At least he won't be on the road as a learner." He sat rubbing his hands together.

"You and Josh have spoken about it! Shouldn't that have been me and you?" My nostrils flared.

Andrew just sat there silent at my reply, which definitely must be a first; I used to get answers back until I backed down, he was always right or thought he was. I took a deep breath and looked at Josh. He was on his knees; he clasped his hands together in the praying position begging me with his eyes again. I couldn't resist.

"OK... OK, you can get up Josh, but I'm warning you, if you have one accident the bike goes."

"Thanks, Mum." Josh jumped up and hugged me tight.

"Is that all, Andrew?" I was stern now.

"Erm... well, yes, for now." Andrew stood up and grabbed his coat and shoes. I saw him wink at Josh through the mirror; Josh gave him the thumbs up. Men!

I shut the door behind him, thank God for that.

"Right, I'm going for a bath. Josh, you have school tomorrow so you best get ready for bed and just because I said yes, it doesn't mean I want to talk about it until I've got my head round it. OK?"

"Yep, that's cool." He hurried off to bed. I wonder how long this good behaviour lasts.

Chloe smiled at me and my raised brows.

"Fancy a little night cap after your bath, Mum?" Chloe was very intuitive.

"There's nothing I would like better, Chloe, I will be half an hour. Make mine Baileys on ice, please."

"OK, then I can tell you all about James." She grinned to herself.

It was obvious Chloe had fallen for this guy, I didn't know much about him and it looks like tonight was going to be a long night.

11

This was the day, it had finally arrived. I arranged to meet the man who I have been chatting to online. We were going for lunch; this was a distraction to help me through the day as later I would be arriving at Mr and Mrs Summers country house party. To go though I still had to find out what my password was supposed to be, I had the invite but that wasn't enough.

I arranged to meet Christopher at a family restaurant in town. I was quite nervous, but didn't mind as I knew Ellie was going for lunch with a friend too. I met Ellie at the bar and she stayed with me until my date arrived.

The restaurant was full as normal. It was a popular place and reasonably priced. The menu was mainly an 'all you can eat carvery' with an assortment of puddings. It was brightly lit, supporting an oversized bar area and dark wooden tables. Freshly cooked meat odours circulated around the room and the staff was rushing about cleaning and resetting the tables.

I'd spent all morning pruning myself; this wasn't for Christopher, but for later. Christopher was my alibi, even though I was only meeting for lunch; Ellie thought I was with him until the night hours too.

"Polly?"

"Hi, I take it you're Christopher." I shook his hand accompanied with a big smile.

"Pleased to finally meet you, would you like a drink?" He smiled back.

"Please, could I have a glass of tonic water?"

Ellie popped over and said her hellos and then left me and my date to it.

He was tall and slender; I noticed he had quite hairy hands in my mind this must mean he had a hairy chest to match. Christopher was dressed in jeans with a knitted cream jumper and long black overcoat. He wasn't my normal type of man, but then with my history maybe I don't have a normal type.

As the time went on I found out quite a lot about Christopher. He had his own security firm and he worked for large, well established companies across England. His main love was horse racing; he had three race horses and even bred a cup winner. His ex-wife ran off with an extremely rich man involved with exports. They had a marriage for nine years and were childless; the horses became their child replacement. Christopher went on to announce that he was looking for a lady who wasn't swayed by money and possessions, in his words 'I'm hoping to meet a normal woman to share my life with'. I really don't think he realises how complicated women can be, if it's not financially, it's certainly emotionally.

Strangely, I began to notice Christopher watching Ellie on the table behind us. I found this a little annoying; he was supposed to be here for me. She is beautiful, but also louder than most when she opens her mouth, so I put it down to that as she craves attention.

Ellie and her friend came over to say their goodbyes, gave me one of her 'go for it winks'. Christopher noticed and laughed, she always knew how to embarrass me. Maybe if it wasn't for George, these two should hook up.

At 2pm Christopher said he had to go back to work, he had a big job on which needed finalising for today. He offered me a lift home; I declined as I still needed to purchase a few things for tonight's event. We hugged and he kissed me softly on the cheek.

"Call me, sometime." Then he left.

The meeting went well, it seemed a little formal, I didn't hold my hopes up for him and me to be an item and he made it obvious he was too preoccupied with Ellie.

I nipped home to find my clothes for the evening. I still hadn't had my password, so was beginning to wonder if it was worth the effort. Then there was a knock at the door.

"Polly Perkins?" A small man carrying red roses stood on my door step.

"Yes." Thinking these was from Christopher.

"Can you sign here, please?" He handed me a clip board.

I signed his papers, he nodded in approval.

"Thank you, bye." I closed the door holding the flowers.

There was a little envelope attached to the bouquet. I put the flowers in water and opened the card.

'1 for sorrow, 2 for joy, 3 for a girl and 4 for a boy, 5 for silver...'

"What the hell is that supposed to mean?" Confused, I read the card out loud over and over again. The only thing I could relate to was magpies, as kids my mother said this rhyme and related it to the birds. If you only saw one bird, you had to salute it to dispel your bad luck, hence 1 for sorrow. I researched the rest of the rhyme on the internet.

1 for sorrow

2 for joy

3 for a girl

4 for a boy

5 for silver

6 for gold

7 for a secret never to be told

8 for a wish

9 for a kiss

10 is a bird you must not miss?

As I searched more, there were various different connotations to the rhyme, with births, deaths, christenings, hell and the devil. I stuck to the one I knew, but it didn't give me the answer to who these flowers were from, but I had my suspicions as the rhyme stopped at number 5.

After safely dropping Josh off at his grans for a cinema, fun filled night and Chloe at her best mates house for a Halloween party, I headed home for a much needed warm in the shower. As I got home, a small parcel stood on my door step. It was a day of surprises. I opened the parcel, which was addressed to me, in front of my open fire. Inside was a collection of items and a hand written note.

"Wear these tonight, don't be late, I will personally greet you… GS."

Oh God, I inspected each item, I had a black decorated mask which was only for the eyes. I put it on; I felt like Dick Turpin and chuckled. The next was a pair of long elbow length satin black gloves and lastly a satin large black hooded cape with red lining. I wore all three things together and I felt and looked a right tit; I left them on and took my photograph from the mirror and sent it to Gabriel's mobile with a caption, 'Do I have to wear this before I arrive or after?' He replied straight away, obviously angry, 'BEFORE AND DELETE THE PICTURE FROM YOUR PHONE NOW!!! A car will pick you up at 7pm don't be late… Gabriel.'

'Wow Gabriel keep your hair on! Jesus, I thought it was a Halloween party and you said there are fancy dress costumes there so why do I need all this now?' I pressed send.

'Just do as I ask… PLEASE… GS.'

Not the reply I was after, I knew I wouldn't look out of place, it was

Halloween, kids and adults would be dressed up everywhere.

Surprisingly, 7pm came around very quickly; I examined my weird outfit, peeking out of the window every second for my so called lift. A black car pulled up, it had blacked out windows to the rear and all I could make out was the driver, dressed in a black suit coat. I ran upstairs for my small (money, keys, lipstick and phone) bag and checked the street to see if the coast was clear for me to escape. I took a deep breath, feeling very anxious about going on my own. I stopped, I only knew Gabriel and I got my mobile out.

'I don't know anyone; I think I'm going to decline your party invite… Pol.' I clicked send.

'Don't do this to me, Polly. You will be fine, I'm in the car outside your house… GS.

SHIT! So I knew I had to go, otherwise he would come and fetch me, then the neighbours would talk and that would take some explaining.

I locked my front door and took huge strides to the car and got in beside Gabriel. The driver set off as Gabriel turned to me. He cupped my face and kissed me deeply making my feelings dance all over the car. He slowly slid his hand over my breasts; he undid my blouse buttons and felt my erect nipples, the tingle made me groan softly. Gabriel kissed my face working his way towards my neck; he blew warm air down the back of my neck, tantalizing my skin as he slid his hand up my skirt towards my warm inner thigh. I breathed deep and rapid, gently he touched my pants, stroking my pussy and a throbbing desire inside me grew. He softly circulated his hand over my silk undies, just using a finger to feel around my panty line, he edged underneath a tiny bit and twisted my pubic hair making my groin thrust in need. I wanted him now; I wanted him to feel inside me, to insert his manly fingers up to my want, desire and need.

"We are here, Sir." The driver spoke.

"OK thank you, Charles." Gabriel pulled away from me.

"You need to compose yourself, Polly."

"What! Well, thanks but you started it, Mr Summers."

"Not now, Polly, just hurry up. Have you got your invite?" His face was stern.

He could tell by my face I had forgotten it.

"For God's sake, Polly! Right OK, you will have to come with me round the back. Charles, can you drive to the back of Lick Penny Lane, please?"

"Yes, Sir." Off we went.

"But if it's your party why can't I just go through the front door with you?"

"God woman, everyone brings a ticket or you get turned away, it's very strict to stop gate crashers. If I do that everyone, will kick off and not pay their membership and I can't give out special rules for certain people, it would be chaos."

"Membership? But I haven't paid." He was making me nervous now.

"Yes, I know, on your first event it's free and if you don't like it you don't have to come again. Now quit the questions, have you got your secret password?" He got out the car nodded to the security guard and marched off.

Great, thanks a lot, Mr Big I AM Summers!

The back entrance was dimly lit, the guard stood before the huge wooden studded doors to the house.

"Good evening, Miss." His voice was sharp and well spoken.

"Good evening, Sir."

He shook my hand "Password, please."

Damn the bloody password! I really had no idea what it would be; I quickly racked my brain for the answer. It took a lot of courage and effort for me to come here alone and without my ticket. Casting my mind back to the roses and the note I answered.

"6 for gold?" I said with a pained expression as I wasn't sure.

"Thank you, Miss, in future remember your invite." He stood a side and opened the door.

"I will do, thanks," I took a deep breath and entered the house.

"Welcome, Polly, Gabriel told me you were at the back entrance." A slim lady dressed in a white cloak and mask greeted me, "Do come with me, I will help you choose your outfit for the night." She led me to a side room.

The back room was beautiful, with subtle lighting it was dressed in white and gold. A warm fluffy carpet covered the floor and heavy gold Draylon curtains covered the windows. There was a walk in wardrobe, various dressing tables which were all white too and a wonderful collection of ball gowns hung to one side on a rail.

"Polly, for tonight you will be known as Miss Scarlett, our identities are hidden for confidentiality and safety. I know who you are because I'm Mrs Summers. Gabriel asked me to look after you." She placed her arm around my shoulder.

I kind of gathered who she was; the different coloured cloak gave it away.

"I'm glad you're here then because Gabriel left me on my own and I've no idea what I'm supposed to be doing," I looked at her through my mask.

"Right then, Miss Scarlett, I will show you what I'm wearing, this is compulsory for all women who attend, Gabriel said you would be OK with it. Oh… and please refer to me as Miss Frost."

Miss Frost faced me, she slowly undid her beautiful white hooded cloak, her hair was beautiful and I could only see half of her face due to the mask. She slipped the cloak away from her shoulders and to my shock she was fully naked!

12

"Gabriel, don't you blame me! You should have told her."

"I'm not, she will be okay. Just give her a few minutes." He leaned against the door frame.

"What if she goes and blabs to everyone, what if she leaves? What then?"

"OK, I will go in and speak to her; you go and entertain the guests, Miss Frost!" Frost by name, frosty by nature! Gabriel turned the door knob and swiftly shut the door behind him.

"Are you OK, Polly?" He kept his distance.

I just sat there sobbing. Gabriel left the room, and then reappeared a few minutes later with a large glass of wine each.

"Come on, Polly, talk to me." He sat next to me at the dressing table.

He handed me the wine, I drank it in one. I grabbed a couple of tissues and cleaned up my face.

"OK fetch your wife back; I need to speak with her, Gabriel." I composed myself.

He came back with his wife in tow, "Shout for me if you need me," and returned to their guests.

After half an hour with Miss Frost I was ready. I gained few answers and I understood a few things about the night, but not all of it. I was ready to give it my best shot; if only for the chance to be close to the main man himself. I followed his wife into a large room close to the front of the property; there were so many rooms you could easily get lost around here. There were many people, you could tell the men from the women, but everyone wore the same. Only Gabriel's wife wore white. I figured he would pop up at any moment to find out what was said, but he never showed.

Everyone was chatting in a composed way, drinking wines and spirits mainly. There was a large table full of champagne flutes; each one had a strawberry in the bottom. I watched the waiter fill each one, reminiscing my time in the hot tub. I must have given myself away with looking around the room and its glamorous décor when I was approached.

"Hi, I'm Mr Green, are you a newbie?"

"Hello, yes I'm new. I'm Miss Scarlett, pleased to meet you." I nodded slowly.

"Thought so, I can always tell; everyone new admires the nude paintings in here."

"Was I that obvious?" Gosh I must stand out!

"A little, but don't worry, everyone here will help you out; they're a good bunch." He smiled picked up two glasses of champagne and gave me one.

I felt a little more at ease now I had a new friend. One by one the crowd of chatting individuals started disappearing. Until I was the last person there, even my new friend had said his goodbyes. So now what? It felt like you worked on your own, no one was allowed to influence you into anything; it was all free will. This worked for me; I had grown to love my mind these days.

The room was truly amazing. I took one last look at it and drank two more glasses of champagne. I needed to take the edge off my worry. I still hadn't seen Mr Summers, I didn't even know his stage name, as his wife told me 'you're not allowed to use real names here', it's one of the rules.

"Miss Scarlet?" It was Gabriel's wife.

I spun round "Hi, erm, what do I do now?"

"That's why I came to fetch you; we will proceed to the next room. I thought you would follow the others, I guess not," she giggled, "Come on, it's time to start." She held out her hand.

This felt weird; I was holding Miss Frost's hand as we left the room of beauty. She was obviously looking after me and whilst being a touch over nice.

We entered a rather large dining room. Still holding hands, I now began to feel uneasy and vulnerable. Everyone stared at us as she closed the door. Before us was the biggest banqueting table I had ever seen, another masterpiece to fit the Manor. All the seats were taken, apart from two. I presumed they were for me and Frosty. In the middle of the table sat a man in a deep purple cloak and mask, Mr Summers and the empty chair next to him was for his wife. The other empty seat was right next to him, surely they don't want me to sit with them? Surely someone new had to sit at the very end?

"Welcome, do come and join us." Gabriel had stood up, Frosty lead me to the table front opposite the empty seats.

Frosty left me stood there and sat at her throne, he was still standing.

"We welcome our newest member, Miss Scarlett." Everyone applauded.

I quickly scanned the table. Gold goblets were full of wine and crystal decanters supported more wine if needed. I calculated thirty seats and all eyes were on me.

"Miss Scarlett is replacing our old Miss Scarlett. After the sad loss of one member; we have a happy meeting with another. I do hope you will all make her feel welcome and introduce yourselves as the night progresses." Everyone raised their goblets as a hello gesture.

Gabriel stood up, everyone followed him. He poured some wine in to a goblet and handed it to me, "Drink with us."

I took a sip, everyone else downed their drink, so I did the same. Summers and his wife lead the way from the table; the other guests followed him in a line. Yet again Miss Frost grabbed my hand and they lead me into another room. This house was a maze of rooms and doors, I felt so out of depth, if Gabriel wasn't there I would have bailed by now.

The entire house was dimly lit. Some rooms had wooden panels for walls, others had wallpaper and paintings. The ceilings were very high, crystal chandeliers hung in every single one. There were open fires in the majority and dozens of red sofas. I yet had to explore the upstairs rooms and in my mind I was trying to work out where the hot tub room was hidden. That's when my head started swimming. I felt dizzy yet serene.

As I was lead through room after room, I failed to notice some of the guests had dispersed. Still feeling relaxed and strangely warm, I allowed myself to be guided in to a smaller room and then we stopped. This room was not like the others; it was carpeted and had huge scatter cushions instead of seats which covered the whole floor, there was no fire place and the lighting was red. At the side of the room was yet another door, this had a lit up sign above it, it currently said Vacant. We entered that room.

Gabriel turned to me and smiled. He took me from Miss Frost, towards a large stone table set in the middle of the room.

"Don't be afraid, after this you can roam the house at your will."

I turned back to look, that's when I noticed there were only five of us. His wife smiled at me, then the other two guests which were men, grabbed each of my arms and lifted me on the table. Gabriel and his wife stood by the side of me as I was lay flat. My head was spinning but I still noticed the two male guests stood back away from the table and crossed their arms as a signal of 'OK'.

Gabriel came closer to me, his wife stayed put, I really didn't understand what was happening, but I felt too relaxed to care. He reached down towards the tie on my cloak; he undid my tie and the few clasps that held it together. I was naked, only sporting my mask. He bent down to me and kissed me gently on my lips. He slid his hand from my cheek and gently trailed his fingers lightly over my nipple down over my stomach and through my pubic hair. His wife joined him at the other side of the table. She mimicked him by first kissing me, then placing her hand on my body, feeling my breast and sliding her hand through my pubic hair. I was too bewildered and scared to move, at the same time I secretly loved being caressed and adored. My tigress was bought to attention; the hardest thing was I knew I had to keep still. Then the shock came.

Gabriel stood back and joined the guests with folded arms, yet Miss Frost stayed put. I realised what was going to happen, maybe this is her control of the situation, she already knew about me and Gabriel meeting up, this was all about power. I had a choice, either stay or run, but I so wanted Gabriel, maybe I had to allow his wife first go, that way I could have him. But I knew I could refuse, but did I want to?

I looked at her and watched her slowly untying her white gown. She let it fall to the floor, her body was beautiful and she had an hour glass figure and perfect rounded breasts. Women weren't my thing, but I was willing to make an exception in order to be with him.

Miss Frost kissed me, I blanked her out and in my mind she was Gabriel, she gave me a long deep kiss which tingled my being. She gently began to lick all the way down my neck and teased her warm tongue around my erect nipples. I arched my back in excitement. She was so soft and playful and tickled my stomach with her fingers. She grabbed my hand and placed it on her fabulous breast; I stroked and carefully twisted her nipple making her groan for more. Then she took back control and waved at the men to join her. All three stood behind her as she pushed my legs up so my knees were bent and relaxed my legs to each side of the table. Now all four of them could see my aching need, with my legs parted she teased her fingers inside me. I groaned with want, she moved very slowly inside me feeling my wetness she teased another finger in and began to kiss my inner thigh. One of the male guests began stoking Miss Frost's behind, whilst another was caressing her breasts; she was obviously loving it, now all the attention was on her.

"STOP… I can't do this." Gabriel was obviously peeved.

The men stood back as Miss Frost composed herself and spun round to Gabriel.

"Outside. Now!" She shouted at the two men.

The others swiftly left the room and all the attention was on Gabriel. Miss Frost took her mask off, before promptly placing her hands on her hips in a fit of anger.

"What are you doing? You're revealing your identity!" Gabriel was not amused.

"So… she knows who you are, maybe she needs to see me and realise not to mess with my husband!"

"Just because you're mad, doesn't mean you have to be reckless for God's sake!"

"Reckless! Tell me Gabriel, why did you stop the ritual? Do you have feelings for her? I want to know and I want to know NOW!"

He paused; she stood there her eyes penetrating his body, like she had some kind of super power to make him speak the truth.

"No, that would be absurd! It's you; maybe I don't want anyone to touch you!" She could tell he was lying, but softened anyway. Miss Frost melted.

Even though I was in a weird place, my head spun and my limbs refused to work, I could tell she was a very beautiful woman, one that has just revealed her identity to me.

"I hope so, Gabriel, I remember the last Miss Scarlet, now we don't want a repeat of that, do we?" She redressed herself and stormed out the room.

13

I don't know how long I was asleep for but when I came to, I quickly realised I had been left all on my own. I felt completely violated and scared, how dare they just leave me! I jumped off the stone table, readjusted my hair and gown and headed for the Gothic wooden door. I took a deep breath to compose my burning anger and left the room.

Thankfully, there wasn't anyone in the adjoining room, which had hundreds of scatter cushions, nor could I hear any voices. I hope I wasn't left in there to rot, what if everyone has gone and I'm stuck in this house! I began to panic; I needed to get home and fast.

I walked through a maze of rooms some lit some not, still no one was around. I discovered a small flight of stairs; these were very different to the ones at the front door. They were very basic and normal. The wooden steps began creak a little as I climbed to the top. This must be a different side to the house; my internal sense of direction failed to guide me as my inner tigress had taken over and seemed to know where she was going.

I heard mumbling coming from one of the rooms off the landing. The door was slightly ajar; I was desperate to have a look, so I trod carefully to stop the floor from squeaking. I really don't know why I was so shocked, after what I had been through, this was tame. The effects of alcohol were wearing off nicely, my body felt more like my own again, I hated the lack of control I had on the stone table.

There were naked bodies everywhere, men and women only wore their masks. Candles lined the walls and incense burned filling the room of a musky aroma. From what I could see there was no furniture, just a very huge man made bed which almost filled the entire room. The ceiling was covered in mirrored tiles, so I just looked up as it was a better view.

It was a free for all affair. I saw women with women, men with lots of women, men changing from woman to woman, all lying next to each other, having sex together, touching and feeling whoever they wanted to. I searched the ceiling for Mr Summers; I couldn't find him amongst the slithering groaning bodies. I caught sight of his wife, yet again she had three men touching and feeling her from all angles… so where was Gabriel?

Someone grabbed me.

"Don't make a sound, it's me," Whispered Gabriel, "Come with me."

He lead me back down the stairs, my inner kitty was not amused with his behaviour and lashed out at him when the coast was clear.

"What the hell has just happened to me? And why didn't you tell me you organise sex orgies?" I slapped him hard stinging his face.

"Right… shut up and come with me!" He demanded grabbing my arm.

"NO, I'm not going anywhere with you, you're really taking the piss out of me and I'm done here." I snatched back my arm and stood away from him.

"OK, you leave me no option." He scooped me up into a fireman's lift; all I did was kick and scream for him to put me down, which was a total waste of energy!

Being upside down my robe slipped, my hood was covering the majority of my face and all I could see was the floor as we went through the different rooms (carpet then red tiles then black marble). I made a

91

mental note of this so when I escaped his clutches I had my internal map. This also took my mind of the fact that my naked backside was in full view for anyone to see and I felt utterly stupid and exposed.

I got carried out of the back door, I felt highly embarrassed and my cheeks flushed instantly as the security guard who welcomed me chuckled at my expense, Gabriel sharply told him not to let anyone know he had seen us go out the backdoor. He replied with a 'Yes, Sir' and closed the door behind us.

He took me over the grassed area of the garden, down some moss covered steps and over freshly dug ground. At one point I even thought I saw a worm pop his head out of the soil for a snigger and crafty old trees were bending their branches for a closer inspection, they were taunting me attempting to slap my bum, as we entered the woodland area at the bottom of his garden. I was beginning to think this torture would never end; suddenly we came to a stop.

He placed me on the floor in a crumpled mess. I straightened myself, covering my body as much as I could; I looked at him as tears of relief trickled down my cheeks. Gabriel stroked each tear away from my face and tenderly moved my hair around my ears. He held me close, allowing me to bury my head into his warm chest; accepting that I needed time to recover, he gently rested his head on mine, it felt like we were melting into one.

The full moon flickered through the aged trees giving us enough light to gaze at each other. I moved slightly away from him, he glanced at me, my mind quizzed at why he appeared so soft and reassuring especially at what he had lead me in to. Gabriel gave me a melting smile, of which I returned immediately. I wanted to stay like this forever but knew that he would never be mine.

Our minds simultaneously relocated our bodies to the floor. We sat underneath an old oak tree on crisp golden leaves. We gazed at each other for a moment, trying to take in all our emotions, Gabriel lovingly stroked my hair and trailed his fingers down to the contours of my lips before affectionately kissing me, pulling me closer to him than ever before. He dissolved all my fears, I felt warm and important to him. He kissed me deeper with more passion, my being followed his every move, until we both lay under the tree fully naked in our own little world.

His hand caressed my curves that were highlighted by the moonlight, stimulating my senses and my womanly needs. Gently he kissed my erect nipples and tickled my stomach making me arch my back in shock. He grabbed my hand and placed it on his erection, guiding me to what he wanted. I srtoked him softly feeling his throbbing desire, trailing my fingers in to his pubic hair and gently cupping and pulling his balls making him moan for more. Gabriel grabbed my head and lowered it on to his erection; I moistened my lips and slowly kissed his swollen tip before tasting his manhood in the depths of my mouth. Groaning, he pulled back and gently pushed me back to the floor carefully he separated my legs and kissed my inner thighs, sending spasms around my body. He softly blew his warm breath around my exposed temple; aching for him to enter and worship me. I grabbed him sharply on top of me. With my draw bridge open he thrust himself all the way not leaving an inch out. I let out the biggest wolf cry before he pulled back and reentered, again and again. Our bodies exuded heat, I was about to explode... then we both did, into a thousand pieces until we collapsed into each other, broken but serene. Neither of us moved, our energy had gone and our breathing was still rapid. That's when we heard voices.

"Quick, put your robe on." Gabriel threw me my attire.

We both dressed quickly hoping we wouldn't be caught. He led me around the woodland round to the front of the house, he definitely knew where and what he was doing, like he had done this before. We entered the house from a small side door which incidentally took me to the room where my clothes were.

"Get dressed; I'm going to get my driver to send you home. If you see my wife, tell her nothing. I will wait outside for you just in case she makes an appearance." He slid his hand under my robe for one last feel of my breasts.

"OK, stop it now or I will take you home with me and hold you captive."

"Hmm I like the sound of that," He winked at me and closed the door behind me.

Our woodland encounter had flushed my skin and also ruffled my hair. I corrected my hair and face first and lay my clothes out to change. Before I had the chance to change, I felt a tingle as our moist explosion trickled down my legs, I looked in the mirror, my tigress was purring perfectly I scowled at her and headed for the toilets. I hung my robe in the exact position I found it and retraced my steps to make sure I hadn't left any evidence of who I was then joined Gabriel.

"Going so soon, Miss Scarlet?" It was Mr Green

"Yes I'm afraid so, family commitments." That was quick for me.

"That's a shame, I was hoping to spend some quality time with you tonight, maybe next time then." He shook my hand, as if I had just agreed to a business deal.

"Mr Green, how are you?" Gabriel appeared from nowhere.

"Good thank you; I was just saying my farewells to Miss Scarlet." He was sharp tonged.

"Jolly good, Mr Green, now if you will excuse us," Gabriel grabbed my arm, "Your lift awaits, Miss Scarlet." He swiftly escorted me out of the house.

A big black car was waiting out front; Gabriel whispered to the driver then pushed me inside.

"What's wrong? Why are you being so nasty?" I said. His attitude annoyed me.

"Not now, Pol, I've got to go before the wife catches me." He slammed the door.

As the car rolled down the drive I looked back, but he'd already gone to join the party. That's when my thoughts over took me. Events of the evening came flooding back. I must have experienced so many strange emotions yet my mind kept returning to only one. Our time in the woods felt so right, I knew we both felt the connection between us. I felt special to him, as his desire to have me to himself and the way he protected me from the others was so comforting. So what made him turn all cold and callous on me? That must be his wife, it could have been her voice in the woods, knowing that I bet he's got to keep her sweet now and now I feel envious. I don't want him with her or the other women and that's just where he has gone, to join the orgy, I just don't understand men!

The driver pulled up near the pub that Gabriel had picked me up from. He must have heard me sobbing as he offered me a tissue, I nodded in thanks I was unable to speak then I set off for a five minute walk to my house. Hopefully, that was enough time for me to get my act together before facing Ellie and her hundred and one questions.

14

Two weeks had passed and not a word from the wonderful Mr Summers. I had kept myself hidden from the world, giving me the chance to heal my wounds and nurture my lost soul. After writing many lists that mainly ended up in the bin and countless cups of tea, I finally decided to write Gabriel a letter.

Dearest Gabriel Summers,

Due to a change in my circumstances, I shall no longer be attending your arranged events at Golden Gates Club. Sorry for any inconvenience this may cause.

Yours sincerely,

Miss Scarlet

I sealed it, labelled it then set off to post it.

One the way, I decided to stop off at my favourite cake shop. I purchased four of the biggest cream and jam doughnuts for tea and grabbed a take away latte. I scrambled out of the shop, it was always a busy shop and customers travelled miles to buy their finest cakes. On my through the crowd I noticed an advert in the window.

Lodge For Rent.

The Peak District. Hidden in Blue Bell Woods.

Rentals all year round.

Set in a beautiful woodland area.

The Lodge boasts a wooden outdoor hot tub.

Hot water heats the Lodge via a wood burning fire.

2 Bedrooms. Very cosy and comfortable. A chance to get away from it all.

ENQUIRE WITHIN.

I fought my way back in to the shop and proceeded to queue up again; this is what I've been looking for, a place to escape to.

The manageress handed me directions and a phone number, I booked there and then for the coming weekend, I thought I might even ask Ellie to join me for a night, with a couple of bottles of wine and a couple of board games, it could be fun. Pleased with my find, I headed home, itching to tell Ellie.

It was edging towards late November and the air was getting chilly. I packed my weekend bag with winter woollies, my trusty dressing gown and fluffy slippers. Ellie had agreed to come with me for the first night, but she had plans with George for the Saturday night, so I packed plenty of books and my laptop in case I needed a few games of solitaire.

Ellie had brought a couple bottles of wine, made us a garlic and mushroom pasta mix and supplied a family sized chocolate gateaux for pudding.

With Josh and Chloe safely en route to be with their dad, Ellie and I jumped in the car like excited puppies. We chatted all the way down, putting the world to rights, singing songs and Ellie's favourite subject, talking about sex. I tried my hardest to avoid her interrogating questions, then to my horror she divulged something which I had firsthand experience of.

"Polly, did you know, there's talk of a secret sex club that runs in town? You can't join you have to be invited!"

"No... no I didn't, tell me more." I shifted in my seat glad of the fact

I was driving, so I didn't have to look at her.

"Well, George was told in the local pub last week that you have to be rich or highly educated with some kind of status."

"Really! Well, we won't get invited then." I tried to make light humour out of the situation.

"Oh, Polly!" She laughed. "I wouldn't want to go anyway. Folks are saying if you don't comply with the rules you have to leave town and if you don't then they murder you, but they make it look like an accident. Their special gathering aims to protect the people involved, so they shut you up. That way no one leaks the location and people involved."

"Bloody hell, Ellie, do you think it's true?" I was shocked at this information.

"I don't know, but can you remember Grace?"

"No, Grace who?" Now I was panicking.

"The school Governess at your Josh's school, the posh one who bought and sold property abroad." Ellie's voice got louder.

"Not really, but did she dress really nicely, in designer clothes and drove a brand new Audi?"

"Yes that's her, did you know her?"

"Not really, I met her at Josh's parents evening a couple of months ago; in fact she sat next to me." I really didn't like where this conversation was going.

"Well, apparently she was a sex club member and she quit. She got asked to leave town or face the consequences. She refused to leave but then ended up in a car accident; someone had tampered with her car, which nearly killed her. She moved after that, her excuse was she had more promising business in America so she relocated." Ellie hardly took a breath.

"That's awful, Ellie, poor woman. Do you think it's true? And who was it exactly who told this outrageous story to George?"

"Well, that's a mystery, because George won't tell me, he said if he tells me that, they could come after him also."

"And now you've told me… great, Ellie! Thanks a lot, I hope we don't get blamed for this leak of information, you mustn't tell anyone else, if this story is true we could end up in a hell of a lot of trouble." Now I was stern but also shitting myself.

"I won't, I've only told you, but the thing is, now I keep walking around analysing people wondering if there a member." Ellie chuckled.

"Oh, Ellie! Anyway tell me about our plans tonight. What do you fancy doing first?" I needed to change the conversation quickly.

"Polly, it's got to be the hot tub, I've already got my costume on under my clothes."

I turned and smiled at her, if she only knew the truth, in fact I'm glad she doesn't. I realised I really had to be careful; it wouldn't be long before Gabriel would get the letter and then they would come after me! And how do I explain that one to my family… even more so Ellie, she knows about the group and how they operate, I wish I had never posted it now, or did I post it? I can't quite remember.

We pulled up at the edge of Blue Bell Wood. There was a designated spot for car parking, we had to abandon the car and get to the lodge on foot. I felt like we had been car booting hanging our belongings around our bodies in large quantities, Ellie had obviously brought far too much, but I didn't have the heart to say no.

We reached the lodge and collapsed everything we were holding simultaneously.

"Thank God for that!" Ellie shouted so loudly the birds in the trees flew off.

I unlocked the door and dragged all our stuff inside. It was beautiful, all of it was made from tree trunks sliced in half to make the walls. The furnishings were pale greens and pinks, comfortable sofas were soft and squashy, lined with crocheted cream cushions. Candles burned exuberating sweet smells of lilies set in a row on the wooden fire place.

"Wow, Polly, it's amazing, let's make a fire first before it gets too cold." Ellie leaped for the fireplace.

"Hold on, Ellie, look there are instructions on the coffee table."

"OK, what do we do?" Ellie was eager as ever.

We followed the instructions step by step, located the wood, got the fire lighter's and the paper. We sat and watched the fire spring to life before unpacking our things. Even though it was a two bedroom lodge, we decided it would be fun to share a room together and it would keep us warmer.

After setting up the quaint kitchen, we headed for the hot tub. It was already on and warm, it looked divine with fairy lights placed around the closet of trees and tee lights glowed on the edges of the tub. A couple of small outside lights which were attached to the lodge outside wall illuminated the tub perfectly. With glasses and bottles in hands we plunged in to the warm bubbly water with a big sigh of relief.

"You've done well here, Polly." Ellie gave me her seal of approval.

"Thanks, I would like to live here, it's so peaceful."

"Only if I can live with you, this place is made for sharing." Ellie jokingly demanded.

"OK, it's a deal." I laughed.

"Anyway, how much has this cost you? Have you come in to money or something?"

I spat my drink in the tub, I need to think and fast. This place wasn't cheap and Ellie could find out for herself the exact price, she always fancied being a detective, I just call her nosey.

"No, it wasn't cheap, for two nights it's cost me five hundred pounds." I was too scared to look at her reaction.

"WHAT!! Bloody hell, Polly, were on earth did you get that kind of money from?"

I'd not told Ellie about my money and after today's conversation in the car I thought it would be best to tell her a lie.

"Well, this is why we're here, to celebrate. I won the lottery last weekend, not the jackpot but I got most of my numbers up."

"Oh my God, Polly," Ellie screamed and jumped on me for the tightest hug ever. "How much did you win?" Ellie tried to compose herself with wine.

"Erm well, if I tell you, you have to promise me you won't tell anyone. Ellie, that means not one soul."

"I swear, Polly, I won't tell a soul, how much?"

"I won quarter of a million (that was a big fat lie) or thereabouts," I sank my nose in my wine glass to avoid her stare.

"That's bloody fantastic; I'm really pleased for you. Is that why you quit your job?" Ellie was now prying.

"No, I'd had enough and needed a change." Another big fat lie from me.

"Oh well, that's dead lucky, what are you going to spend it on?" Ellie was on one now.

"I'm not sure yet, this break away came first and the rest, I'm not a hundred percent sure yet." That bit was true.

"I bet I can help you spend it."

"That I don't doubt, Ellie." We laughed and hugged again, I was relieved that I pulled it off.

The rest of the evening was fantastic. Ellie and I played scrabble, this was Ellie's version of scrabble so all the words were sex orientated and strangely I won. We devoured the pasta, drank all the wine and just chilled in front of the log burning fire. There was no television or internet and the only phone signal we got was on the front porch.

It wouldn't be long before we would be retiring to bed. I was a little saddened that George would come and fetch her in the morning, I'd really enjoyed this one on one time with my best friend, she definitely knew how to lift my spirits.

My only hope is that Ellie keeps her mouth shut about Gabriel's parties. If this got out I would be in the firing line, if only I could tell Ellie the truth, that way I know she would keep quiet to save my skin, but I just can't tell her. The letter; I almost forgot! Did I or didn't I post it? I found my bag and started sifting through it; I had a big bag full of nothing so this could take a while. Ellie joined me in the bedroom.

"What are you doing, Pol?" She caught me.

"Nothing, I thought I'd lost my car keys." I quickly replaced the few items I had taken out.

"Shall we go to bed now, Polly, I'm whacked." Ellie flaked on the bed.

"Yep, let's get some sleep." I quickly shoved my bag under the bed; I would have to look again in the morning, as soon as Ellie had gone.

15

The Lodge was peaceful once again. Ellie had left an hour ago which gave me time to wash the pots, hoover the floor and give the bathroom a once over. I made myself a brew and stoked the newly lit fire to get the flames going.

I sat on the shaggy rug and emptied the contents of my bag; the pile looked as cluttered as my life. I had household bills, lip glosses, a hair brush, chewing gum, random till receipts, five screws and several different flavoured tea packets.

By the looks of it, I must have posted the letter to Gabriel, frustrated I decided to get some fresh air around my brain cells, so I wrapped up warm and headed into the woodland to kick my logic into action.

The winter sunshine began peering through the trees, enticing me to glance up at the magical forest I was engulfed in.

"Ouch!" I began puffing and panting, I had fallen over and cut my knee open.

I dusted my stinging hands and started to raise my trouser leg towards my pulsating wound. I had drawn blood, nothing too serious, but my cut was full of dirt and sticky blood.

"Would ya like a hand with that, Missy?" A stranger offered me help.

I looked up at the owner of the husky Irish accent, he towered over me and in an instant he smiled, producing a perfect set of white teeth. I could tell in his eyes he wanted to help, but I couldn't speak as my lips were permanently glued together to stop my emanating screams.

The stranger bent down to my level and looked hard at my knee.

"I can patch that up for ya, Missy, can you walk? My log cabin is just a few metres away." He stood and offered me a hand to lift myself up with.

"Yes, yes I think so." I took his offer of help.

He wrapped my arm around his waist and gently he put his hand under my arm, together we hobbled to his cabin.

It was beautiful and well cared for. He had made the outside very homely with hanging baskets, lanterns, bright plastic butterflies and wooden, hand crafted bird boxes. At the side of the cabin was a small log store, full of freshly chopped firewood with climbing plants all over it. The inside, however told a different story. It was very basic, a small table with two chairs and a leather sofa. The floor was covered in a patchwork of hessian rugs. There were no ornaments or pictures, just an old cuckoo clock above the fire place.

He sat me on the sofa in front of the simmering fire and placed a large cup of tea in my hands. Glad of the warm drink, it didn't take me long to consume the entire contents of the cup. I felt uncomfortable being in a strangers home, the place felt empty like something was missing.

"Hello, Missy, I'm Ethan, pleased to meet ya." He held out his hand with another smile.

"Hi, I'm Polly, thank you for your kindness." I took his hand.

"You're welcome, Polly; I don't like seeing a damsel in distress. Now let's take a look at that knee of yours." He knelt on the floor with a bowl of warm water, antiseptic cream and a plaster.

I gently eased up my trouser leg peeling the material off my bloody knee. My socks exposed themselves, they were plastered in Sponge Bob characters and feeling embarrassed I flushed crimson.

"I like your socks, Polly, do ya have square pants to match?" Ethan chuckled.

"Ha ha, very funny, I can assure you, Ethan, my pants are anything but square. I need a large size of round to cover my backside."

"Miss Polly, I didn't notice your womanly cushion earlier, maybe I should ave a look at your 'size of round'." He smiled. "Now come on, let's get your leg all better."

Ethan made me blush once more, just red upon red grew on my face. Noticing my discomfort he returned to my injury and was so gentle with my knee; he cleaned all the dirt, dried the wound and placed a plaster perfectly.

"How's that for ya, Missy?" Ethan sat back and admired his handiwork.

"That's brilliant, Ethan, thank you ever so much. How can I repay you? Actually, how does dinner tonight at my Lodge sound?" Christ, I just asked him round for a meal!

"Polly, that would be great, I would love to come. Now shall I walk you back or do you know your way back?"

"I will be fine, Ethan." I stood up, not amused by being kicked out.

"I've got to get back to work, Polly; I'm not kicking you out. I just need to do my jobs and then I can be with you for... seven?"

Yet again I felt stupid. He obviously clocked my annoyance and endeavoured to put me straight.

"Oh, I'm sorry... so you work in the forest?"

"That I do, Missy. I live and work in the forest."

"That sounds fabulous to me, maybe you can tell me all about it later...seven's fine. Thanks again, Ethan." I smiled as I made my way out. I only got a little way in the woods.

"POLLY!"

I stopped and turned around.

"You definitely ain't got a large size of round!" He winked.

Not knowing what to say I just smiled, turned on my heel and returned to my Lodge.

I felt quite spritely having just met Ethan. He was a bit older than me, very tall with curly dark blonde hair and big hardworking hands. To say I came here to get away from the clutches of Mr Summers, Ethan had certainly taken my mind off him brilliantly.

The living room floor still looked a tip from the contents of my bag, so I decided to quickly sort all the rubbish out and keep only the important stuff. Feeling optimistic about the night ahead, I thought it would be best to spruce up a bit before finding something suitable to cook for later.

I took a shower and protected my knee by tying a plastic bag around the wound to keep it dry, that's when I noticed how hairy my legs were. I checked my pits they were the same and my undergrowth… well, it was very over grown. It's time to get rid of the crap and start again.

I defuzzed my body, which took forever and then I washed and conditioned my hair. Finally, I applied a mud based face mask. I had let myself go after the Halloween party, I just couldn't be bothered. The last thing I needed was to look beautiful, it was my 'stay away from me look' but it obviously didn't faze Ethan.

Standing naked in front of the mirror I felt the purr of the pussy cat within, she was ready to pounce, but this time I was holding her back. I turned the best I could to have a good view of my rear. Not convinced that I'm not a 'large size of round', I took out my mobile phone and started clicking away in many different angles. I would view these later after the dinner menu had been set.

Luckily, Ellie did over do the food; I had a bottle of wine left, half a chocolate gateaux, two tins of chunky meat soup and a full baguette. So that was the menu set, not much choice but it was better than toast.

It was around five o'clock when I finished styling my hair. I sifted through my clothes, now wishing I had followed Ellie's footsteps in packing for every eventuality. The best I had was my black leggings and a cream knitted jumper that rested just below my womanly pillow. I smothered myself in perfume and added just a touch of lip gloss which I found in the depths of my bag. As my hair was drying naturally it was curling at the bottom, I didn't have a hair dryer on me, and I left it simple and put a black plastic head band in, scraping my hair away from my face.

That was it, I was nearly ready. I lay the table with the supplies from the Lodge. I placed a lit candle in the middle with the bottle of wine, sliced baguette in a wicker basket and a few wild flowers I had found around the lodge. It looked perfect, not over the top and very homely. All I needed now was my guest. It was half six so it wouldn't be long and I was getting strangely nervous.

There was a knock at the door. Blimey, it was quarter to seven, Ethan must be eager. I opened the door and there he stood with his ear to ear smile yet again.

"Ethan... please, do come in." I smiled back, feeling his coloured butterflies that have decided to relocate to my stomach.

"Thanks, Miss Polly." I ushered him to the sofa.

"Do you mind if I take my shoes off?" His blue eyes pierced my skin.

"Not at all, go for it." I liked a man with manners.

"Hope you like ma socks, Polly, I wore em special like."

"Ethan, they're fab!" I chuckled. "Looks like we have something in common." I was amazed at the square pants all over his feet. "Would you care for a glass of wine?" I held out the bottle.

"No thanks, could I have a cup of tea?"

"That's two things we have in common, be right back." Wow! Ethan was very similar to me.

I made him a strong English brew in the largest cup I could find and sat with him in front of the fire.

"So... Ethan, how come you live and work in the woodlands?"

"Ahh well, twenty years ago I had a wife. She became pregnant

107

and…"

"And what?" I was intrigued.

"She… well… she died in childbirth." He looked down at the floor.

"Oh God, Ethan, I'm so sorry." I felt really bad for prying. "So you have a child?"

"Nope… he died too, one day I had everything, the next I lost my whole world." He nervously twitched his toes.

"I don't know what to say, I'm sorry, I shouldn't have asked." I felt stupid yet again.

"No, it's fine; it was a long time ago. That's why I'm here. I needed to get away from it all, but I liked it that much I decided to stay. I still go and see my brothers every once in a while, but I've got used to the solitude and the forest is a great healer."

"That's why I'm here, to get away from it all and to try and find some sense of direction. I try my best, I write lists, try to make changes, bend my own set of rules a little (maybe a lot) but nothing works." I felt comfortable explaining this to Ethan.

"This is the best place for it, Polly, I hope ya come back and visit again." I could tell he was genuine.

"Oh, I will, I might even buy one of the hidden Lodges if they were to come up for sale."

"They can be a tidy price, there's only six privately owned ones in the whole woods, the area itself is owned by a wealthy man from the next county," Ethan sipped his tea, "I work for him doing maintenance and security."

There was another knock at the door. I looked at Ethan, he looked at me. Who would be knocking on this door at this hour?

"Aren't ya gonna answer it, Missy?"

"Who do you think it is?"

"You won't know until you answer it." Ethan was direct.

Who on earth could it be? Maybe it was Ellie and George, Ellie really didn't want to go this morning, maybe she's brought George here for the hot tub. I got up feeling positive it was her.

I opened the door; it definitely wasn't Ellie or George.

"Polly, I need to speak with you, are you alone?"

"Gabriel! What on earth are you doing here? How did you find me? And what do you want?" My words tumbled out faster than my mind could think.

Gabriel pushed his way through the door.

"It's important, Polly. Oh hello, Ethan," Gabriel turned to me, "I see you've met Ethan; he looks after the grounds for me."

"Good evening, Sir," Ethan held his hand to shake Gabriel's. Gabriel declined.

"Am I interrupting something here?" Gabriel clocked the table with the wine and place settings.

"We were just having dinner. Ethan helped me in the woods today, I hurt myself and he found me and patched me up. This is my way of saying thank you." I was stern.

"Oh… well done, Ethan, the thing is, this isn't a good time, so if you don't mind?" He held the door open for Ethan to leave.

"Right ya are, Sir. Bye, Polly." Ethan left with his head hung low.

"WHAT THE BLOODY HELL ARE YOU DOING?" I was well pissed now.

"I need to talk to you… NOW!" He grabbed my arm and pushed me on the sofa.

He stood over me with his hands on his hips; his eyes were wide and his lips tight. Steam was coming out of my ears, how dare that bloody man just barge in to my space and take over and throw my guest out! I was furious.

Then he put his hand in to his jacket pocket and pulled out a document.

"We need to talk, Polly… it has to be now."

I deflated. Oh God, the letter, it's bloody followed me!

16

I sat open mouthed at Gabriel. I couldn't believe what I was seeing. I felt so bad about Ethan, I decided to get this over and done with and go and find Ethan and maybe I could persuade him to return for a dip in the hot tub. First I had to get my bollocking out of the way, after all that's what he's here for, to read me the riot act.

"Polly, can you please tell me why you have sent this?" He was very composed.

"Yes, actually I can. As it states in the letter, I don't want any more involvement with your stupid club. In fact I never wanted any involvement in your stupid, controlling club. So now you know you can show yourself out." Proud of my stand to Gabriel, I relaxed.

"It doesn't work like that, Polly, you can't just leave. If you insist on doing so, I have to take it to the board and they don't take kindly to people just leaving, especially when you've already attended one of the events." He was still stood square.

"I don't care! You had no right to violate me like that." I was angry.

Gabriel crouched down in front of me and took my hands.

"Polly, please I want you to stay." His voice was soft again.

This is the part of Gabriel I hated; he somehow seemed to know how to push my buttons. I smelt that smell of Gabriel, his touch affected my every pore. Instantly, my anger disappeared and my body ached to hold him once again.

"Polly, I'm talking to you… are you listening?" He kissed me gently on the cheek.

"Yes, I don't understand, why me? And why are you here now?" I was intoxicated by his essence.

"Because, Polly, now is the right time. You're not at home so no one can see me, no one can hear us and no one will bother us."

"OK, what do you want to talk about?" I felt vulnerable now.

"Me and you?"

"What about me and you?" I waited for a response and got none, "There is no me and you!" That worked.

"OK, look, you can't leave the club. Oh and someone saw us at the party and snitched to my wife, so I've had to worm my way out of that one, she thinks you're staying, so you see you can't leave." He didn't move a muscle.

"So you want me to stay to save your sorry ass, because someone saw us?" I couldn't believe my ears.

"Basically, for now it would be really helpful, there's nothing to say you can't leave after this issue has blown over." His voice was virtually begging.

"Best I will do is have a think about it and when I get back home I will contact you with my answer." I felt in power again.

"Polly, there are things you don't know about me, things I don't want you to know, or should I say things you'd be better off not knowing, can't you just trust me?" He sat with me on the sofa.

What things? And how did he know I was here? I was so drawn to this man, how could I refuse? I knew this conversation would be going round in circles, I knew he didn't want to give up and accept a slap on the hand from his wife, but it didn't feel like it was enough to convince me otherwise. He was the one who invaded my life, the one who instigated our meetings, our feelings and our love making. I just wished he wasn't so God damn delicious, I wanted to devour him, here and now.

I glanced in to the burning fire, watching the flames dance freely in flashes of warm colours. Ethan's plastic butterflies were painted the same warm colours. I looked over at the table that was set for my new friend. The candle had half burned and the flowers had wilted. How could I have pushed such a lovely man away? Then I remembered it was Gabriel that threw him out.

Ethan had felt real hardship in his life and is just looking for a new chapter to begin. I felt bad, knowing I had to make a decision and quickly, but to choose was still hard. My whole being wanted to give in to Gabriel, but I felt a pull towards Ethan, I needed a plan.

I reached over to Gabriel, kissed him softly on his warm moist lips. I cupped his face with my hands and gently slid my fingers down his neck, over his chest. He responded by pulling me closer, slowly teasing my nipples over my jumper, they became erect instantly. I felt my groin moan for more, my inner tigress stood up for more attention as he gently kissed every inch of my neck. His tongue trickled down to my neckline making static waves over my body. His hands crept up my jumper tantalising my skin with every stroke and then in a split second decision, I moved away from him.

"No, not now, I came here to get away from you, not to have more of you."

"I've missed you, what's to stop us here? It's just you and me." Gabriel looked puzzled.

"You know what, Gabriel? I've missed you too, but you can't be the only one to pick and choose when we meet up. If you really were that bothered about me, you would leave me alone and let me get on with what I'm doing here instead of totally pissing me off!" He had definitely rattled me.

"Shame, Polly, but OK I get it, I will send for you soon, the wife's away in France for a few days over Christmas," He stood and headed for the door.

"Great, it would be nice if it were a mutual decision." I held the door open for him.

"I make the decisions, Polly and by the way, your hair really suits you."

Gabriel gently stroked my backside on the way out; my kitty cat was not impressed that I allowed him to leave, she screamed down my ears; 'No, don't let him go'. I ignored her, I had to keep strong, there was someone else I had to see and I intended to be there in half an hour.

It had turned dark outside so I went to see Ethan armed with my trusty torch. I took my time as I didn't want another part of me scratched, broken or twisted. The forest was almost still, apart from the crunch underfoot and the odd owl hoot. The darkness curled around me, putting all my senses on edge, the smell of soil and pine invaded my nose as I tried to remember the exact route to Ethan's cabin. I knew once I had smelt the freshly chopped wood that I would be close.

My mind started to wander as I allowed my intuition to guide me. Gabriel... my children... Andy and his bit of fluff... Ellie and George... how I had come to this point in my life, I will never understand. Then there's the money, all that lovely money just sitting around in my bank account doing nothing. I knew I had to get out of the maze I had put myself in to and I knew that my children came first, the last thing I wanted was anything to happen to me because of the Gabriel situation, so job number one was to protect my kids and safeguard my life.

My nose caught the smell of fresh wood, as I moved a little more through the trees I could see Ethan's cabin illuminated by the glow from his living room. I turned my torch off as I approached his home. I didn't want to spook him and I was feeling nosey so I thought it wouldn't hurt to creep up and peer through his window.

I crept up to his window, dodging the crispy leaves under foot; I controlled my breathing and gave myself a minute to convince myself it was OK to spy. Quietly, I edged myself to a dark corner and slowly moved just my head round the window to have a look.

I saw Ethan sat at the small table with his back to me, I could tell he was concentrating on something, something intricate and wanting to know more I shuffled to the other window, for a better indication of what he was up to. I felt nervous as I was closer to him this side of the cabin; I secured my feet to the floor and very gently bent round for a peek. It was amazing, Ethan was painting on a canvass and he was painting butterflies. I was mesmerized at his work, I enjoyed watching him so much that I didn't realise he had seen me.

"Polly, please come in don't stand outside peering through ma window." He twisted his body round to face me, with a big smile on his face.

"Oh shit, you've seen me, sorry." I felt like a naughty school girl for being caught.

"It's OK, Polly, I knew ya were coming."

"You did? How did you know?" I was puzzled.

"I just know, right let's get the kettle on." He headed for the kitchen.

"I'm sorry about earlier," I shouted as he went, to avoid eye contact. "I didn't know he was coming and I didn't even tell him where I was, so God knows how he found me."

Ethan came back armed with tea and cookies; he gestured for me to sit down and sat next to me.

"Look, I don't know what's going off between you both, but he's ma boss… and I have to do as he says, If I lost ma job, I would lose ma home too. So Polly, it's none of ma business." He dipped a cookie in his hot tea.

"OK, well I feel the need to explain myself. I've known Mr Summers a few months, since my partner left me for a younger woman. It's not something I planned… but to cut a long story short, he pursued me and there isn't any relationship as such." I hoped that would be enough.

"Like I said, it's none of ma business, Polly." He shuffled uncomfortably on his seat.

"Tell you what, why don't we go back to my lodge, the food's still OK and I bet you're starving?"

"That I am, Miss Polly. I will just get cleaned up and we can set off if ya want to?"

"It's a deal, Ethan." Pleased with his acceptance, I smiled.

Whilst Ethan was getting washed up from his painting, I couldn't resist having a look at his work. He was very talented; there were lots of wildlife pictures, mainly of butterflies in various colours and sizes and the odd tree picture in the different seasons. Then I came across one sketch drawing of a half naked lady. I was quite shocked, but it was beautifully done. Her face wasn't showing and she had twisted her body in to a side view, my brain was quizzing who this woman was.

"Arh, do ya like em, Polly?" Ethan caught me engrossed in his work.

"Oh yes, Ethan, they're fantastic!"

"I bet you're wondering who the lady is." He was reading my mind.

"Well, I wasn't going to ask. She's a very good model, or was it by memory?"

"Not memory, I was asked to draw her. Mr Summers brought her here. That's a draft he has the original painting." His words tumbled out as if it was a frequent occurrence.

"Oh I see, so how many exactly have you done?" Now I was interested.

"Quite a few, he hangs them up in his Manor house." He was still unfazed.

Little did Ethan know, I had seen all his paintings, they were magnificent and definitely caught my attention during that night at the manor. My tigress pricked her ears up, I knew what she wanted, but laying here naked in front of someone I hardly knew seamed out of character. I fought back her feline attack, but not enough will power saved me this time.

"Ethan, will you paint me?" Shit I'd said it.

"You, Miss Polly?" He looked amazed.

"Yes, or am I not young or pretty enough?"

"Polly, you're beautiful, why would you say that… it's just, I only paint naked women for Mr Summers. The paintings are like trophies for him. He has had many women and before he ends his affair with these women, he has them painted. I've been doing it years and do ya know, he's never had one done of his wife!"

"Just how many women, Ethan?" Anger washed over me.

"Why are ya getting shirty? Are you having an affair with him?" He was cross.

"Kind of. God, Ethan I need to get him out of my life, but he won't let me go." Tears started flowing, my anger has diminished.

"Well, that's obvious, coz I ant painted ya yet! Come on, Polly, don't cry, I will help ya and if ya want I will paint ya. Can we do it another day though? I'm looking forward to that supper." He was comforting me with a cuddle.

I nodded in acknowledgment, still shocked at what I had just found out, I felt completely crushed.

17

Ethan successfully had me laughing again, so we began our trek back to my lodge for a late bite to eat. My trusty torch wasn't needed, Ethan knew the way in the dense, dark woods. I found this quite exhilarating, allowing a man I had just met to keep me safe. He had a strange effect on me; I knew I could trust him, he was like my guardian angel.

We never sat at the table. We ate our soup and crusty bread on our laps and found a little space for the chocolate cake, along with a strong cup of tea.

We chatted for hours, sharing our thoughts on the purpose of life. Ethan told me he believed everything happens for a reason whether it is good or bad. That one path leads to another and all our souls are connected to each other. He regretted a lot of his actions and decisions and explained that we are what we choose to be. Through his sad loss he made lots of changes and told me not to take everything for granted. He was very interesting with his mindset, he also admitted he realised all this after his wife and child died and he wished he could turn back the time and start all over again.

Ethan gave me a lot to think about, I knew he was trying to give me some guidance without actually telling me what to do. This was Ethan's way of helping me then to my surprise he stopped in mid sentence and looked at me. He asked if I had ever had my fortune told and as I had never had it done, Ethan then reached in his pocket and pulled out a deck of tarot cards.

"These are only for guidance, Polly, I can show ya the path, but it's up to you to make the choices ya need. Do you understand, Missy?" Ethan was absent mindedly shuffling the cards.

"OK, this looks like fun, how long have you been a tarot reader, Ethan?" This man amazed me.

"Ten years now, I needed to find out ma path so I started going to fortune tellers hoping for someone to tell me what I should do with ma life. I was lost, Polly. Ma wife was ma life, so ma life was gone. I gained nothing from all the readings I had, none of them could tell me what I should do. Then one day an old woman knocked on ma door selling lucky heather. She told me she could feel ma loss and that to find ma path I had to heal myself first and then apply ma skill to others, so the next day I looked for a teacher in spiritual arts to teach me to heal and to read."

"So… does this mean, when I fell over in the woods and you rescued me, which was not by chance, that we were supposed to cross paths? And is that why I find you so easy to talk to… because you're a healer?" I found Ethan was becoming alluring.

"Ya got it, Miss Polly, now do ya want this reading?" His deep Irish voice was hypnotising me.

I cleared the table, placed a new candle in the middle and lit it. Ethan laughed and told me it wasn't witch craft and asked me to put the main light on. I declined and insisted that this was much friendlier. I was hoping I wouldn't cry and if I did it would be easier to hide with candle light.

Ethan shuffled the cards, I watched, amused by his speed with such big cards; I could tell he had been doing this a while. He then passed me the pack and asked me to shuffle. He told me this was my subconscious actually choosing what he was going to read for me. It was me picking the information that was the most important and was the area which needed addressing.

I tried helplessly to shuffle the huge cards; this I found was harder than it looked. A few cards dropped from the pack, those ones Ethan kept to one side and he called them 'important' as they had jumped out. He went on to explain that it's very common to find it a struggle with the cards and not to worry. Ethan asked me if I wanted to cut the pack or leave it how it is, so I left it.

"OK, let's have a look what ya got." He started flipping the cards, the ones which jumped out he placed in position first.

He laid them down in a set format.

"Right, Polly, remember this is only guidance, everything I tell you is what you chose to show me. Hopefully you will get a bit of clarity and make the correct decisions for you to move forward in your life." He was very professional, his wonderful Irish accent disappeared.

"Ethan, can I record this on my mobile, just so I don't forget what you said?"

"No problem, Polly, when you're ready we shall begin."

Ethan proceeded to explain which cards meant what. He told me the basis of what the reading was about. This made me nervous.

"OK, Polly, your past cards are telling me you underwent a major change in your life. Your whole world fell apart and you had to find the strength to rebuild it. As you walked on this path of rebuilding your life, you came in to an opportunity of money and wealth. This helped you in one area of your life, but not the area you wanted." Ethan paused and looked at me.

"Yes, that's correct." I was astounded; he got all that from three cards.

"The middle cards represent what's bothering you now. You've given me the lovers and the eight of swords." He paused again. "You feel trapped in your love life. I feel your mind and heart aren't matching up

119

making you make decisions from pure emotion at the time. I see a man, whom you don't see eye to eye with and your past hurts are controlling you, rather than you taking control. The first card in to your future is also a relationship card. This man is a real charmer and I feel this card is already integrated in to the present." He paused again.

"That's also very true, Ethan." A lump filled my throat.

"Shall I carry on?" He noticed my pain.

"Please do, I need to hear this."

"OK, the next few cards are your future. These are events that can be happening now, or are crossing your path within the next four weeks. Then the rest are up to a year. " He looked at me for approval to continue.

"Right. OK, I'm ready." I took a deep breath.

"You have the Knight of Cups, the Devil, Two of Swords, Temperance and the Page of Cups. You've been so desperate to fill your emotional hole that you've got to a point which you need to make a decision, but you're unsure of what to do for the best. You've given in to temptation and through this have felt locked in to a certain man whom you feel is unobtainable. Be careful of dark paths, they are so easy to walk down and really hard to get away from. I do feel you will see this man again. You need to separate your emotions to gain control, time away pondering about your decision shall give you clarity and the ability to plan and decide your next step. This man, Polly, is Mr Summers, but you know that, don't you?"

"Yes, it's him alright!"

"He's the man that swept you off your feet, the charmer?" Ethan tilted his head.

"Yes, he has. He showed me how to be a woman again." I looked down in shame.

"OK, well as I've said before, sometimes you have to walk down the wrong path to get to the right one; I feel this is what you're doing." Ethan looked at me with sadness.

"OK, so things happen for a reason?" I felt optimistic now.

"Yes, even if it's so you can learn more about yourself and what you want. Shall I carry on?"

"Please do."

"There is another man entering your life, a new love and relationship which you so desire. It's one that's firstly built on and then friendship and then trust. I don't see any greed or temptation with him; although I feel he could get intertwined with the other man if you allow it and both your feelings will be severed. You have a new start though, but this new start actually begins with you or someone around you that you love being ill or hospitalised. Don't panic, it's not life threatening but through this event, changes to your pathway have already started. There's also a pregnancy in the family or with someone very close to you. This will urge you to move forward again, I feel you've been putting this off for some time now and this pathway will help you make the changes around you. I can see some type of business brought in to action. An idea you have had in the past will spring in to action, this is also at the same time you move house."

"Move house! Pregnancy! Illness! Ethan, will I sort all this mess out? And do you think my daughter will get pregnant? Because, if she did I would have to move house!" I sat open mouthed at his final words.

"Polly, I'm not sure about all that, but one final thing. You will have the last laugh and it begins with a blue butterfly."

"What begins? Will I get the last laugh? Or is it when I can actually make and stick to any of my decisions?" I was desperate to know more.

"When you have made a decision, that's when the blue butterfly will come. It's clarification that you've made the right choice." Ethan's eyes were quizzing my ticking mind.

"Thanks, Ethan, you've given me a lot to think about." I kissed him gently on the cheek.

Ethan looked at me with his bright blue eyes and smiled. He gathered his cards and placed them back in his pocket. I didn't want him to go; I'd not even asked him if he wanted a dip in the hot tub. By the look of it, I wasn't going to get that chance.

"Thanks, Missy, I will be off now. Work as normal tomorrow." Ethan fastened his jacket up.

"OK, Ethan, are you sure you don't want a fresh brew?" Sadness overcame me.

"Another time, Polly, look after yourself, you have a beautiful heart... don't let him destroy it." Ethan looked drained.

"OK, Ethan, take my number. You still have my body to paint." I smiled. "That is if you still will?"

"Course I will, Miss Polly," His pearly white teeth gave me a proper display.

Ethan wrote my number down in a small note book from his jacket. I gave him a firm hug before watching him disappear in to the dark of the night. Ethan had a warm presence about him and a very caring nature. Now that was the type of man I needed in my life and according to Ethan I was about to meet someone who filled my emotional holes. This meant all my internet dating was a waste of time, all the blokes I had previously met were not the one... hmm I wonder, if that man I'm supposed to be with, could be the man who's just spent the last three hours with me.

18

My weekend had come to a close. I began packing my things feeling utterly miserable at the thought of going back to everyday life. I sat on the sofa, gazing at the table where Ethan had given me that lovely reading, reflecting on the words passed during the night. He gave me a lot of insight. I was deliberating if any of it would actually be true. I knew now that I would be consciously looking out for those blue butterflies.

I hurled my things in to my car. I had less than I came with, as Ellie was the one who insisted bringing the whole world with her. I sat at my steering wheel and took a deep breath. I saw a small card on my window screen fixed down by my wiper blade. I got out and grabbed the card, I was about to throw it away thinking it would be some kind of 'get rich quick scheme' when I noticed a small drawing of a blue butterfly on the reverse. It was from Ethan, scribbled on the opposite side was his mobile number. This put a smile on my face as I realised my new friend was here to stay.

The morning was crisp and cold, so I had to drive home at a steady pace, which gave me lots of time to sing to my favourite tunes. After listening to my 80's rock CD over and over again, I got bored and stopped at a village bakery for a ham salad roll.

I sat down with a pot of earl grey, waiting eagerly for my food, I was starving. That's when I noticed everyone looking at me. Customers froze and stared at me for a split second, even the staff put me on edge. After about thirty seconds everyone resumed back to their worlds and left mine.

I made a swift escape to the toilet, wondering what was out of place. I twisted and turned in the mirror to find the culprit. I found nothing; I had my hair in a ponytail, my big winter coat and thermal boots on. I was no different to what anyone else was wearing; maybe it was because I wasn't a local villager. Happy with my assumptions I returned to my seat.

The waitress brought my freshly made ham roll this time with a smile and then I realised she wasn't smiling at me. She was smiling behind me at who ever had just walked through the door.

"Good morning, Sir." The dainty voice came from a young waitress.

"Good morning, Amy." I recognised that voice and spun round instantly.

He gazed at me, but never spoke. The aroma of his aftershave trailed with him along the café, as he made his selections from the menu board, he searched with his eyes for a place to sit; there were plenty tables available but strangely he chose to sit with me.

I carried on eating, aware that the whole world had its eyes on me again. Still he never spoke, apart from my very loud heart beat we ate in silence. It must have been the longest bite to eat in history. I felt totally in the spotlight, the café was deathly quiet amongst the odd whispers.

"I need to show you something, do you have a couple of hours now?" He spoke softly.

"No, I've got to get back." I was quick to the point.

He sighed, "Polly, this will be my last request. I promise I will leave you alone to rethink your position after this."

"Fine, two hours exactly, make them count." My voice raised a notch, a few heads popped up.

"Polly, will you be quiet! Let's go." He demanded, so I followed, avoiding a scene.

Once outside the bakery café shop, I felt relieved and able to breathe again.

"That was awful, do you know everyone? I never realised you were so popular, I wonder why?"

"Sarcasm is not your strongest point, Polly. Anyway what do you mean… why?" His eyes narrowed.

"Well, I take you're a born flirt. You have money, status and power and by the looks of it you own all the frigging land, buildings and businesses in this district. So it's no wonder any woman would fall at your feet!" He made me mad.

"Yes, well, that maybe true, but I like a challenge and I've definitely got one with you!"

"What are you trying to say? There's no challenge because there's never going to be an US!" He infuriated me.

"Wait and see, Polly, just give me two hours, that's all I ask." His voice softened.

"And if I don't?" I decided to test the water.

"If you don't, then you will always wonder why. You will always ask yourself what could have happened. Those questions eat away at you, Polly and I know they probably already have." He stopped walking and looked at me for an answer.

I covered my face with both hands and took a deep breath. He was right, I would have asked myself all those questions and I couldn't help but over analyse every single situation I found myself in.

"OK, where are we going?"

"Good. I'm glad you're seeing sense, follow me in your car and we're going to the Manor."

Oh God, the dreaded house of sex, that was the last place I wanted to go, but he was right if I didn't go I would never know what he wants me for.

It only took half an hour to get to a secret parking location near the house; I left my car there and got in to his. I had hundreds of questions for him, but somehow I knew this wasn't the time or place. My mind cast back to Ethan's card reading, Gabriel fit perfectly in to my story, but what if Ethan was lying? What if Ethan wanted me for himself so he tried to plant that seed of doubt? Or is Gabriel the Devil card, the temptation that Ethan was referring to? And then there's the blue butterflies which was for confirmation, there were far too many questions in my head.

Glad that I had sorted my quizzical mind out, I relaxed a little. It wasn't that Gabriel didn't know me; he had seen me inside and out! I just didn't want to go back in that house; at first I thought it was the golden gates to Heaven, now I know it's the golden gates to hell.

Gabriel drove to the back of the house. He parked up, got out and opened my door.

"Come on, I've got something to show you."

I didn't reply. I did as he asked and followed him in to the house. Gabriel led me around the back to a small locked door. He located the key from his jacket pocket and unlocked the arched door. Once inside he locked us in and put the light on. I was amazed; the room was small and decorated in dark greens and browns. There was a huge floor to the ceiling book case and many photographs on the walls, each one had a name attached to it.

"This is my history, Polly; feel free to ask away, you've got fifteen minutes. I don't want to spend all my time in here whilst I have your undivided attention." Gabriel sat at the leather bound desk.

I scanned the walls, all the people in the pictures were men and they all had a title. Sir Lucas Summers stood out, he looked like Gabriel the most and not far off his age. There were older men all with the surname of 'Summers' and a couple of them were called Lord! I now realised

Gabriel had a very big title against his name and there he was his own picture on the wall, Lord Gabriel Summers! Now I felt out of depth again.

I froze on the spot, I think this was what Gabriel wanted, to show me not to tell me. I was unable to talk, shock overcame me.

"Do you understand, Polly?" He walked towards me.

"I think so, I'm not really sure. If you're a Lord, why didn't I know about it?" I turned to face him.

"Well, I'm not a Lord yet, but soon I will be. Most people in the surrounding villages know I'm wealthy, but not many actually know about the blood line. I just get fickle people wanting to be nice to me, not many are actually themselves around me."

"So what's your wife then?" Still I didn't fully understand.

"She's horrible, Polly; she's a selfish, evil manipulator!" His face changed.

"No! I didn't mean that… what's her role?"

"She's the controller; she's the one with the title. Her family are all dukes and duchesses. To retain the heritage and keep all the estates between our families we were told we had to marry. It would have been nice to find the right girl, fall in love and live happily ever after, but neither of us was given that choice." His head lowered.

I could feel his sadness penetrating my body, his sorrow and pain was running through my veins. I grabbed him and took him in my arms and held him tight. I felt his sobs on my shoulder and wondered how I could have mistaken this man for the Devil. It was clear his wife pulled the reins in his relationship and she was having the time of her life. Where did that leave Gabriel? What did Gabriel want?

I could feel his vulnerability. I stopped myself from asking anymore questions. Gabriel was right, there was a lot I didn't know about him, I understood why he had a need to control our meetings but it still didn't answer my questions on how many Miss Scarletts there had been. According to Ethan he had painted many of Gabriel's ex lovers, so what happened to them? And would I be the next victim to sit on Ethan's couch naked.

Gabriel moved away from my grasp and held my hand. He led me to the small green leather sofa at the back of the room. Gabriel took a deep breath then jumped on me. In a flash he was ripping my clothes off and I was returning the gesture.

We were both fully naked, sliding about on the couch, his hands touching every inch of my skin. He kissed me deeply using his tongue to explore my mouth making my back arch for more. He grabbed me under my back and lifted himself up.

Gabriel moved back and took hold of my legs pushing them up to the ceiling; slowly he trailed his tongue from my mouth across my erect nipples over my stomach and down to my purring kitty. He kissed me softly between my thighs before gently teasing his tongue through my pubic hair. I moaned and thrust for more; Gabriel repositioned me and slowly twisted the tip of his tongue around the folds of my sensitive skin.

I grabbed the sofa with both hands, my nails dug deep in to the leather as he tenderly entered his tongue inside me. My body was struggling to hang on to my eruption as he teased my secret button in a circular motion. I was bubbling and fighting to hold on to my display of ecstasy. Sweat rolled down my face and trickled on my breasts, all this time my heart was trying to escape my body.

His moans and groans made me worse, my moistness dripped down my legs. I tried to regain control but failed as Gabriel pushed one finger deep inside me whilst still licking my button; I exploded in to a thousand pieces my body tingled through every pore. He very quickly moved away from me and rammed his throbbing desire deep inside my need, making my explosion happen all over again and again until he exploded himself and collapsed on top of me in an exhausted slump.

He kissed me softly; his eyes were soft and relaxed. I stroked his face with a smile. Hopefully, my reassurance would melt his trapped emotions.

"GABRIEL… GABRIEL! I know you're here somewhere, I've just seen your car!"

"Oh God, it's the wife! She's not due back for another six hours. She's been to France with the kids. Quickly, get dressed." Gabriel's soft face turned to stone.

19

Luckily, she couldn't see us as there were no windows in this strange hall of past residents. I dressed as fast as I could, waiting for the next command from Gabriel.

We both listened to his wife stomping on the gravelled path outside the Manor, until the crushing stones became still, we waited and soon enough she must have gone to the front of the house.

"You stay here; I'm going to get rid of her." Gabriel looked agitated.

"OK, don't leave me too long; I do have to get home before the children come back." I wanted to escape.

"I will be as fast as I can, I promise." He repositioned his hair, then left me and locked the door.

I must have sat there for half an hour still waiting to be released. I gathered that if I was going to be much longer, I would have to warn Andy and Ellie that I would be a little late. I got my mobile phone out of my bag and switched it on. My battery bleeped low, so a simple couple of texts would have to do.

I had three notifications, all of them were from Gabriel and he had tried to call me three times whilst I was at the Lodge. A wave of naughtiness came over me, I felt like returning his call especially now he was trying to bullshit his wife, not far from me. I chuckled, if only I were that brave and could actually carry out my bitch side, what a laugh I would have.

I sent my apologising texts to the relevant people in my life and turned my mobile off again. I still sat there, the grandfather clock chimed, it had now been an hour what was he playing at? Then I heard the crunch of the pebbled path again.

Someone was outside the house right next to the room I was in. I stood next to the door and rested my ear up to it; I was trying to find out who it was and what was happening. I heard nothing; I was desperate to cry out but also knew I would blow Gabriel's cover. Then the footsteps disappeared.

Another hour passed and I started to panic, the walls were closing in on me and I was desperate for the toilet. I got my phone out again and decided to send another text.

'Gabriel, I need to go, please release me, it's been two hours now!' I sat staring at my phone.

Then it bleeped and bleeped again, it was Ellie and Andy acknowledging my earlier texts. My phone bleeped twice, my battery had only five percent life left. Worried my mobile would conk out I searched in the desk draws to see if there would be a charger that fitted my phone.

My phone bleeped at last it was Gabriel.

'Sit tight, I won't be long… I'm sorry.'

OK, so he shouldn't be long, I turned my phone off again and quit the search for a charger.

"I know she's here, where have you hidden her, Gabriel?" Angry shouts vibrated on the door.

The stomp of feet reached my room of confinement, someone started twisting the door knob and rattling the door.

"Are you in there, Polly?" His wife was furious. "Gabriel, give me the damn key! I know she's in there!"

"There's no one in there, I'm done with this!" Gabriel was not impressed. "I'm off home!"

"That's right just walk off, you've got no spine, Gabriel!" Her footsteps followed him.

Great, so I'm still here, surely he is doing this as a decoy to get rid of her. I heard a car start up, do a swift spin around and speed off. Maybe this is how he's going to sneak me out. Still desperate for the toilet, I had to use the waste paper bin; maybe if she did open the door and have a go at me, I would throw this all over her in temper.

Feeling bored I started snooping around the draws. I came across a thick leather bound book. In it were all the names, addresses and professions of all the members in Gabriel's sex club. There was even a list of people who no longer attended the meetings. I took a deep breath and started at the beginning.

It dated back years ago, when I was a young girl. I went through all the 'p' surnames just to see if my parents were listed, gladly they weren't. I skipped through a couple of years and started from when I turned thirty. I felt sick; people who I knew and trusted were on there and are still listed as attendees. I carried on searching; there were teachers, politicians, bank managers, sergeants, successful business owners... Ellie's ex-husband and then I found Andy and his wife!

I got my phone out, I had three percent battery left, just enough to take a couple of photos.

I started clicking away at all the evidence, I found a few more people that knew me well and I even found George to be a worker of security. So that's how he knew and that will be why he told Ellie to protect me. Oh God, that means George probably saw me with my ass out! Now I felt stupid and naive.

Angrily, I took the book with me to the leather sofa. I turned to the page of 'quitters'. I was surprised that Andy was on there, his little wife was too so that will be why they moved to another city miles away.

Andy had suppressed them by offering donations. All this was going off when we were together, this will be how he met his little wife, at these blasted parties! My nice side was wearing very thin. I was sick of being exploited and used. Where the bloody hell is Gabriel?

I saved all the photos to my memory card. I took the card out of my phone and put it in my bra. I had a strange feeling something wasn't right and if anything did kick off, all that lovely evidence was stored safely.

I must have cried buckets looking at that book of the damned; I'm not sure why I was shocked when my name was the last insert. I had also been listed as a quitter, so someone other than Gabriel knew about the letter. Oh God, am I going to starve to death in here?

I put the disgusting book back and started snooping further. I needed to know more about this family and how they operate. I came across a few photos of the family together at Christmas and birthdays and a few pictures that had been painted by Gabriel's children.

I tried the other drawers; most of them were full of stationery items, a brandy bottle half drank and some strange powder in a packet. I opened the packet and sniffed the substance, immediately I knew it wasn't legal. I tasted it out of curiosity, if it was what I thought it was, surely it would calm me down for the next hour.

The bottom drawer could have been the worst; in this drawer were newspaper clippings of people involved in freak accidents. These people were from all over England. I relocated the book of members and started matching up accident by date and name. So it was true, if you leave the gatherings, you should be prepared for the consequences! Not all of these people had died, lots had recovered then found solace in other areas and countries, they all shared one thing in common, they were all women.

I'd seen enough, I made a mental note of the newspapers that had covered these stories for my evidence file. This evidence file would be one of revenge. I realised I couldn't take these people on, just beat them at their own game. My fighting spirit turned to life plans running through my head, I remember this feeling when Andy left me and today is the start of payback. I may not have the power yet, but I definitely have the money to give me a head start. Then the powder kicked in.

I lay on the couch watching the huge clock tick minutes into hours. It was now six in the evening and my children would be home, but I had Ellie there to give them some tea. My body and mind felt all calm relaxed, the same as that evening at the party. Unbeknownst to me I had been drugged; I remember how I fell asleep so I tried my hardest to stay awake.

Another piece of the puzzle fitted in to my head. Most of my questions had been answered. One major question was why Gabriel had picked me and why he wanted me to stay. And where in all this does Ethan become involved?

I knew he was involved somewhere, he had already told me about Gabriel's other women of which were all listed in the book of quitters. I couldn't wait to get on my laptop and research all these women, maybe they would speak to me and join in with my idea.

It was now seven in the evening. Knowing it would be dark outside, I felt sure Gabriel would come for me soon. I could hear someone banging about outside the room. I made no attempts to listen or shout for help, I was just worried about which story I would be telling Ellie when I finally got out of this prison.

The person outside must have been tidying the grounds. I could hear branches being broken in half and crispy leaves being swept. I sighed, if this was the gardener, Gabriel couldn't sneak me out as the room I was in overlooked the garden and woods.

I smelt smoke from the debris that was being burnt in the garden; it brought back memories of when Andy and I cleared our garden when we bought our cottage. We had many evenings burning rubbish and garden waste, smelling of stale smoke and sharing showers together before we would embrace ourselves between the sheets.

I did have some happy memories of our times, sadly they didn't last. Maybe his need to explore more sexually led him to this place and its dirty little secrets. I knew know that this would have been the start to us finally drifting apart, just like it's doing to Gabriel and his wife. Thinking about it, I bet this is why Ellie and her husband split, as Ethan said one path leads to another.

I still felt relaxed, even with the cat out of the bag. It was starting to get hot in the room, I started sweating and looked for the radiators to turn them off… there weren't any! I could hear the roar from the fire and debris still being thrown on to it. It cracked and popped and became very loud.

Smoke started creeping under the wooden door, the dark green paint started blistering on my side… oh hell, the door was on fire! Quickly my being came back to life, the effects from the powder had disappeared and replaced with fear.

"HELP, HELP… HELP!" The door was melting away and flames came rushing in to the room in a huge ball!

I picked up my bucket of urine and threw it on the flames; it failed so I ran to the back of the room screaming over and over again. There were no windows so I couldn't escape; the heat and fumes were intoxicating. I lowered myself to the floor for air as the flames curled around the desk and covered it in a sea of yellow. I placed my coat over my hair in desperation to breathe normally without smoke, then I went to the very back corner and lay on the floor.

I started crying, I was going to burn to death or run out of oxygen. The gardener obviously wasn't a gardener; I would just be one of the many burnt paper clippings which I had found earlier.

The smoke wrapped itself around me and squeezed the air from my lungs, my eyes could no longer open and they stung from the black fog. Furniture was still catching fire as I heard the viscous roar of something

135

else which had gone up in flames.

I realised this was my path and accepted I was about to die a horrible death, I curled on my side like a dog with my coat covering me and started to drift, unable to inhale any life.

"POLLY, POLLY... ARE YOU OK?" Gabriel was violently shaking me.

Gabriel had returned too late, I heard the fire brigades sirens over Gabriel's cries... but it was too late, I slipped into darkness, my body and soul faded away.

20

A stream of warmth glowed on my face. I felt loved and secure. I held my hand out to the celestial being, hoping that my journey across to the other side would be quick and uneventful. I was drawn, it felt right and as I was tired of my uphill struggle, I willingly wanted to go. But she didn't take my hand; she had other plans for me. She smiled and gently rested her hand on the top of my head. A tingling, golden glow surrounded my face and weaved its way round my whole body. I felt light and incredibly serene.

It was early January when I finally got home, unaware of what actually happened and suffering from the effects of my prescribed medication, I decided the only thing for me to do was rest. Chloe and Ellie helped me in to bed, as soon as I buried myself in to my duvet; my thoughts returned to my angelic encounter. Knowing I was safe, I slipped in to a deep sleep.

It was midmorning when I finally woke. I carefully twisted my body around to see my bedroom window. This was the first time I had slept at home since the fire. I drew my curtains back wondering what the outside world was up to and a ray of intense sunshine hit my face. The whole street was blinding and decorated as a winter wonderland.

The sun glistened on the fresh snow. Peoples homes looked like ginger bread houses with icing on their roof tops and trees stood proud covered in their new winter woollies. All I could do was look at it from my window, there are only so many windows you can look through before you start realising life does go on.

"Morning... Mum." Chloe greeted me with a hot cup of tea.

"Morning, sweetheart." I smiled and gladly took the tea.

"You've seen the snow then? Josh has gone sledging for a few hours and Ellie and George have gone to the shops for bread and milk," Chloe sat on the edge of my bed looking shifty.

"OK that's fine... what's the matter, Chloe?" I knew her too well.

"I've got something to tell you and I don't want you to be mad." She looked down.

"You're pregnant?" I kept my face straight.

"Yes, how did you know?"

"Call it a mothers intuition, I'm not mad Chloe, in fact I'm thrilled for you both, even if you haven't been together long."

"Thanks, Mum, I love you." She hugged me tight.

"Ouch! Be careful, Chloe." I winced at my burns.

"Sorry, Mum, the nurse is coming today to change your dressings and I've got your laptop here so you can pick a wig until your hair grows back." Chloe's eyes filled up.

"Hey, come on you, I'm still here. It's a good job if I'm going to be a Grandma," I hugged her tight.

"We all thought you were going to die, Mum. Grandma and Grandad came daily but they kept falling asleep next to you. I played your favourite songs on your iPod, Ellie and George just sat and talked to you, Ellie mainly giving you all the village gossip and Josh just kept quiet, I think he was scared. Strangely, Dad came to see you twice a week, he read you stories from the daily papers. You did have two men visit you though and a snotty stuck-up-her-own-arse woman, I've no idea who they were, but I could tell by Ellie's face she knew who they were." Chloe said, obviously wanting me to spill information.

"Can you do me a favour, Chloe?" I sat upright.

"Yeah, what is it?" Her eyes narrowed.

"Get Ellie for me and my mobile, please."

"OK, but your mobile melted in the fire, I've got this though!" Chloe pulled out my memory card.

"Oh, Chloe, thanks! I need a new phone. Here, take my bank card and get me the best top notch mobile you can find. Get a cab as the roads look bad." My money has come in handy at last.

"OK, any particular one?"

"Not really and while you're at it can you find me a wig. I want a black one and make it long."

"BLACK! But, Mum, you're blonde, won't it look odd?" Chloe was shocked.

"That's the idea." I handed her my card.

She grinned and shook her head. I had a plan, this wasn't something that could be done overnight, but I felt like I'd been given a second chance with my life, so this was my time to make my life my own.

"Oh, Mum, I nearly forgot. The hospital handed me this and told me to give it to you when you were feeling better." Chloe handed me a brown envelope.

"Thanks, Chloe. When I'm out and about we will go baby shopping OK?"

"OK, Mum, thanks." She leaned over and kissed me then left.

With Chloe gone, my thoughts returned to the mess I had landed myself in.

I had lots of questions for Ellie and no doubt she would also have lots of questions for me. I got my trusty note pad and began writing down things I needed to know. I needed answers and I needed them fast. If the fire was deliberate then I had limited time before something else would happen.

I began drafting out another one of my famous lists, but this one was very different to all my others, this one included my family and the need to protect them all, especially now Chloe was pregnant.

I heard the door go, it was Ellie.

"Hello, Polly, I'm here. Chloe text me and said you were awake and wanted me?" Her voice got closer.

"Yes, come in, Ellie. I need to ask you something."

"Hi," Ellie stood in the doorway. "I thought you might." She sat on my bed.

"Is George with you?"

"No, he's just nipped to the local to let everyone know you're home safe, oh and to have a beer as well." She puffed.

"OK... I need to know a few things, now I know you will want to know the... who, what, why and when questions, but I have to ask first and I may not tell you anything straight away, you just have to know that in time I will tell you, but not today." I was as clear as possible with her.

"God, Polly, since when did you turn in to a copper?" She was as charming as ever.

"Ha ha, very funny, I'm serious Ellie."

"OK, fire away." She lay on her side facing me, obviously getting comfortable.

I looked at my 'quick questions' list. I started simple testing the water.

"Did you know I'm going to be a grandma?"

"Yes... next." Ellie was impressed by that one (not).

"And Andy came to visit me twice a week?" I crossed the questions off as I asked them.

"Yes... next." Ellie started getting impatient.

"I've told Chloe to fetch me a new phone and a wig."

"BLOODY HELL, POLLY!" She snatched my note book and read each question before looking at me.

"Look, I just need to know." I started crying.

"Polly, don't cry. I'm sorry. Look I will make a brew and answer all your questions. I wanted to do this when you were a bit stronger though. I have got something to tell you though, some good news." She handed me a tissue.

"That would be great, thanks, Ellie." I blew my nose.

"In fact, Polly, can I use this note book? I will number and write the answers on the back and you can read them at your leisure?"

"If you don't mind that would be fab, thanks, Ellie." I shouted as she left the room.

I must have fallen asleep after that as I woke to the evening light trickling through my room. I flicked my bedside lamp on and there on my bedside table were my evening tablets, a glass of water and my note book. I took the tablets to ease my pain and sat myself up for my questions and answer list.

Ellie had done exactly what she said she would, even if some of her answers were short.

No.1 Who found me?

A man called Gabriel Summers, in fact you were in his house and he has a very big house!

No.2 How long have I been out of it?

You've been in a coma for a month, you missed Christmas and New Year but we all spent it with you in the hospital.

No.3 Does anyone actually know what happened, if so who?

I'm not sure, I know Andy does and Mr Summers and his wife. They came to visit you quite a lot but I'm sure they are missing out information. The police were happy with what they told them, it smells dodgy to me. There was another man who came with Mr Summers, he was a bit lush! He seemed very concerned about you and left you a little present too. Not sure if he knew the whole story.

No.4 Did I die?

Yes, you did but they brought you back, I've never been so scared in all my life. Your kids, Andy, me and George were there for you. Then strangely, an hour after you came back Mr Summers and his wife came to the hospital, I'm not sure how they knew you pulled through. We didn't tell your parents until you were stable.

No.5 Will you help me with my plan for the future?

I sure will, Polly. Just say the word. First though, I need to know the whole truth. I know something's going off, I also think the fire was deliberate. I've been studying the Summers and something's not right, Polly. You also need to open that letter the hospital sent you, ONLY I know what is written, I asked them to keep it secret and when you're ready I will tell you why they approached me and not your parents, children or Andy.

I love you lots, Polly, you're my best mate and I'm so glad you're still in my life. Now, open your letter xxxxx

Nervously, I reached for my brown envelope. I took a deep breath and slid my little finger under the seal. I was not prepared for what I saw.

"ELLIE, ELLIE! I need you a minute." I had a sweat on, my mind shattered and my heart thumping.

Ellie burst in my room and she was totally out of breath.

"You OK, Mum?" Chloe shouted from the bottom of the stairs

"Yes darling, did you get me phone?" I tried to keep my voice calm.

"Yeah, shall I bring it up?"

"Ellie will get it, thanks, Chloe." Ellie turned on her heel and retrieved my new phone.

She looked at me; tears rolled down my face Ellie gave me the phone and wiped my tears from my reddened cheeks.

"Come on, Polly, we will get through this together. I'm here for you every step of the way."

"How come Chloe gave me the letter and not you?" I was puzzled.

"Jesus, Polly! Chloe found it in my bag; we have the same hand bag.

She took mine out by mistake and found the letter." Ellie was not happy with Polly's lack of trust.

"Shit. Sorry… Oh God, Ellie, what am I going to do? How on earth do I explain this?" I was distraught.

"Why don't you start by squaring up with me and I will help you find a feasible tale for everyone else?" Ellie was right.

"I can't tell you all the details right now, but I will when I've recovered from this horrible nightmare." I lowered my head in shame.

"I do need to know what happened and why you were there, but I agree, let's concentrate on getting you fighting fit again. There will be plenty of time for the details."

"Yes, you're right, there is something I can share with you. Shall I just come out with it?" Ellie nodded eagerly. "Gabriel Summers is the dad and I'm too old for another baby. Ellie, what shall I do?"

"Right… OK, well, that explains why he was there talking to a private doctor at the hospital. You had fantastic care, all of which he paid for. He was adamant that you had round the clock supervision and all your tests were run by 'HIS' private doctor. Hmm, your call, Polly. What do you want? You won't be on your own, don't forget Chloe is pregnant too." Ellie had given me new information.

Maybe the baby was my safe card. The key to keep my family and I together and to cement my future life in the village instead of having to move away like the other women. This could be my payback time, he won't touch me while I'm pregnant and after I've had the baby I can get to the bottom of all this and return the wonderful invite with my own Halloween party.

"Oh and Polly, this is what that gorgeous man gave you in the hospital."

It was beautiful, Ethan had crafted a sparkly dream catcher made from fallen forest feathers, weaved branches and tiny hand painted blue butterflies.

I started to cry, all this new information overwhelmed me.

"Come on, Polly, you will be fine. Whatever you decide to do with your pregnancy, I'm here for you." Ellie gave me a hug.

"God, Ellie, I'm so screwed. I must be the Devil's spawn!"

"No, you're not; you're like most of us women. We all have our own recipe. You're like sugar and spice and all things nice." Ellie laughed.

"I don't quite think so. You missed a large *dash of crazy* in there!"

"Polly, I do believe you may be right!" We both collapsed in giggles.